Nun of My Business

A DragonEye, PI story

Karina Fabian

Laser Cow Press

MERRITT ISLAND, FL

Laser Cow Press
Merritt Island, FL
https://fabianspace.com

Publisher's Note: This is a work of fiction. Names, characters, places, and incidents are a product of the author's imagination. Locales and public names are sometimes used for atmospheric purposes. Any resemblance to actual people, living or dead, or to businesses, companies, events, institutions, or locales is completely coincidental.

Cover art by Dawn Grimes
DragonEye Logo by Allen Oaks (Len Fabian)
Laser Cow Press Logo by Allen Oaks
Tweet by Tweetgen

Book Layout © 2017 BookDesignTemplates.com

Nun of My Business/Karina Fabian -- 1st ed.
ISBN: 978-1-956489-07-1

Dedication

To veterans, especially those suffering from PTSD. May you find a friend as good as Vern.

May you find as good a friend as Sister Grace!

Contents

*A hoot from beginning to end and thoroughly
enjoyable on every POSSIBLE level!*

Chapter One: My Kind of Nun

When you're an immortal dragon like me, you get to know women in a variety of ways: snacks, bait, treasures, annoyances with high-pitched screaming... You get the picture. Then, after my encounter with St. George, I've gotten to know women in other ways over the past eight centuries: caretakers, instructors, fellow laborers, even commanders.

So believe me when I say there's no woman quite like Sister Grace McCarthy.

Father Rich paused with his hand on the door. "Are you sure you want to do this?"

I glanced up and down the antiseptic hallways, decorated with cheerful art and cautionary signs. Of course, I wasn't sure. Through the slim window, I saw a crucifix affixed to the wall, a reminder to me that service came with pain. Once I crossed that threshold, I'd be at the mercy of a dozen probing hands, under interrogation, and subject to who-knew what humiliations?

"I promised," I finally told my Confessor and my first friend in the Mundane. "Besides, I'm getting paid."

Father shrugged but didn't volunteer to come in with me. I desired neither chaperone nor witness, and he knew it. He did, however, bless me with the sign of the cross before opening the door to admit me.

I arched my neck, settled my wings comfortably, and entered Sister Mary Margaret's Fourth Grade Classroom.

Twenty-three bored children suddenly drew themselves to attention with a collective gasp—some with delight, some with fear. I recognized some from Little Flower Parish; they grinned with delight, and one whispered to her neighbor proudly. This was their chance to get some playground cred. Very few parents were comfortable enough yet with my presence to let their kids "bother" the dragon that attended Sunday Mass, but I knew that wouldn't stop them from bragging that they knew me. One kid regarded me with greedy eyes full of mischief. He had the seat closest to the teacher's desk, which I'd been told was reserved for particularly naughty kids. Today, it looked like he'd been rewarded instead of punished.

By her desk, Sister Mary Margaret seemed less delighted. She held a yardstick in a death grip, and I didn't know if she thought she would use it to defend the children in case I went feral, or to keep her feral class in line. From the stories Frankie Costa told, it could go either way. Beside her was another sister, wearing the habit of the Faerie Order of Our Lady of Miracles. So she had magical backup? For me, or in general?

We'd find out soon enough. Frankie left his desk, took his place in front of me, and raising his paper to reading level, started to speak. "Good morning, Sister Mary Margaret, Sister Grace, and class. My report is on Faerie Dragons. Faerie dragons were created the day after God rested. They do not die, and they do not have offspring, so there is always the same number of dragons. Only the other dragons have gone away, and no one knows why. Vern is the last Faerie dragon that lives among people."

He paused here to wave in my direction with awkward showmanship. A couple of kids snickered, but fell silence when Sister Mary Margaret cleared her throat.

"Dragons worship God just like we do, but they do not have to be Catholic. Vern is Catholic because Saint George converted him."

I did the equivalent of biting my lip. I'd tried to explain the theological nuances of dragon faith until Jerry Costa had finally said, "It's close enough for a nine-year-old."

"Dragons are normally as big as a house—maybe a hundred feet from nose to tail—and weigh as much an airplane. Dragons have one hundred and twenty-eight teeth and can tear apart meat like a tiger. They have two-hundred-and-seventy-degree vision. That means they see everything in this area." He spread his arms to demonstrate. "And they can fly and breathe fire and do magic. They also remember everything and are the smartest creatures in creation."

And now the humiliation.

"Vern is no longer that big or powerful because he lost a fight with Saint George."

Greedy Eyes snorted derisively. "Some drag-on! Beat up by an old guy with a sword."

I stepped toward him and got my face with its 128 teeth up close to Bratty's snot-nose. He jerked stiff and his eyes went wide.

"I lost a fight to a puny mortal who had the power of God on his side. Think about that."

In my 270-degree vision, I saw Sister Mary Margaret start forward, only to be held back by a light touch of the Faerie nun. I thought I caught a ghost of a smirk; if so, that was my kind of nun.

Frankie continued with his report, mixing a few more fun facts about the glory of my kind with some of my personal history protecting the Faerie Pope and fighting against the forces of evil. You know, my glory days stuff. It sounded trite and (pardon the expression) mundane when translated into words a fourth grader could spell, but Frankie finished up before his classmates' fidgeting got too noticeable. They clapped polite-ly, except Bratboy, who was picking his nose. Several raised their hands to ask me questions.

"How long are you staying?" one boy I recog-nized as an altar server asked.

"In the Mundane? As long as God tells me to." I'd already learned the hard way about disobeying God in such matters.

A blond-haired girl asked, "Why can't dragons have babies?"

Another topic I was warned to keep at a 10-year-old level. I shrugged. "We weren't made to have them. I guess God figured seventy of us is enough for one world."

"So you don't have a mom or a dad?"

"Courtney doesn't have a dad," Bratty quit digging in his nostril to say.

"Randal!" Sister Mary Margaret reproved.

Courtney's lip quivered, so I stepped in and answered as if specially to her. "Dragons don't have parents. We were all created at the same time, just seconds apart. So we're siblings. I have thirty-four elderkins and thirty-four youngerkins and one twin. Like you."

She exchanged a surprised glance with her brother who sat two rows back. "How did you know?"

"I can smell the family resemblance."

Another child spoke as he raised his hand. "I read that dragons can smell virgins."

Sister Mary Margaret tensed, but I answered, "True."

From the back of the room: "Sister Mary Margaret, what's a virgin?"

She cleared her throat. "An unmarried woman with no children."

Randal snorted at his desk. "Courtney's mom ain't never been married."

Sister Mary Margaret ignored him, instead answering another child's question about how Holy Mary could be a virgin, but the mage sister approached Randal's desk.

"Mayhaps ye should be bringing your thoughts to God before you share aloud with the class," she suggested quietly.

Randal went pale and pressed his lips shut tight.

Meanwhile, another girl raised her hand high. I took in the scent of hair product and lip gloss that just skirted the school rules for the grade. Addison Lukas. Her name was oft spoken in the Costa household, along with the phrases, "teacher's pet" and "snooty know-it-all" yet Anna Theresa said she was one of the popular kids, even among the fifth graders. I never understood human interaction, but I knew enough to expect her question to have more edges than a magical sword.

"Do dragons sing?"

Before I could answer, I sensed a surge of anxiety—from Sister Grace. Still, near the edge of my vision, I saw her face remain impassive, but I scented the rise of stress hormones and could hear her increased heartbeat. Beneath the long bell sleeves of her habit, she had her fists clenched. Odd.

"No, I don't," I said, distracted by the signals I was getting from my fellow Faerie. Why was that question a gut punch to her?

Taking my hesitation as an invitation to elaborate, Addison continued, "Not even in church? My mother said we should always sing in church. 'Make a joyful noise,' she says. Even if you aren't any good. It makes God happy. Francisco said dragons are the wisest of all creatures. Isn't it wise to make God happy?"

A tangle of emotions surged from Sister Grace. Fury. Guilt... Fear? And now some of the kids were giving Addison the side-eye. There was some context I didn't know but they did. Addison kept her guileless expression focused on me, but the predator in me recognized a kindred spirit. She knew the effect she was having. Meanwhile, Sister Mary Margaret was smiling, oblivious to stress growing in her fellow sister or the building tension in the room. No help there.

I decided to sidestep the issue. "There are lots of ways dragons make a joyful noise, and a lot of ways we please God. Not all of them are a good idea for Mass. And not all of them are appreciated by humans."

"Like fire breathing!" Frankie interjected.

"Like fire breathing," I agreed. "Most of your legends only show dragons breathing fire as a defense or an attack, but in reality, it's a lot more than that. We use fire to communicate, to warm up our caves, even as art. It has a sound to it, too—and to dragon ears, it's an incredibly joyful noise."

I couldn't help but grin. St. George had taken my fire in our epic battle, and it had been one of the most painful things to lose. Now that I had it back (a reward for saving both universes from a dark-elf plot), I felt more whole than I had in a long time. It was also a great way to cure hangovers, something I got more often than not nowadays. But I didn't mention that to the children. Instead, I suggested a demonstration.

The kids cheered.

Now, Sister Mary Margaret reacted.

"No!" she shouted. "I mean... I don't think..."

Sister Grace, too, had broken free from whatever had hold of her psyche. She set a reassuring hand on her fellow teacher's shoulder. "I think there's no harm in Vern lighting the prayer candle, would ye not agree?"

"I'll get it!" Addison jumped up before anyone could volunteer. She seemed as eager as the others, but I'd seen how her lips puckered into a pout just before she joined in the cheering. Someone didn't like the attention taken off her and her scheme.

That was fine. The attention should be on me, anyway. I made a showy display, sending out a narrow, curling tongue of flame to light the wick. After we all said an Our Father (it was a prayer candle, after all), I allowed the kids to come paw at me. I didn't mind being petted, as long as no one rubbed my scales the wrong way. They continued to ask questions, all at once: Did I eat people? (Not lately.) Do I know the centaur that delivers pizza in their neighborhood? (No, but you can invite me over if you order me a large with everything.) Has anyone ridden me?

Meanwhile, Sister Mary Margaret chided them to be careful, to take turns, to not get too close to my teeth, and the like, with mixed results. Sister Grace blew out the candle and put it away. She seemed recovered, but I felt more than saw that she was shaking.

Then, Sister Mary Margaret yelled, "Joseph, no!" and I felt something heavy plop onto my back between my spikes.

"Hey!" I snarled and twisted my head. I'd been saddled!

Some of the kids squealed and backed away. Others moved forward, ready for a turn in case I approved. Joseph froze, stuck between desires.

"But I brought it for my report," he said.

Fr. Rich spat out his soda when I told him.

We were at the Costas', in the backyard, enjoying one of the last warm days before the autumn chill came in with a force. I was there to collect my pay: a huge pot of Rita's special chili, liberally spiced with Carolina Reaper just for me. The kids had been warned away from even breathing what was in my bowl, and Jerry had added one spoonful of my chili to his and had coughed and gasped for a full five minutes. Father looked like he might take equally long to catch his breath.

As he choked and laughed, Rita handed him a dishrag to wipe his spill. As the parish priest, he got invited to the cookouts I had to earn by being a prop for her son's school report. There was no justice in my world.

"Bendito," she cooed, scratching me behind the cheek. "Did you let them ride?"

She was teasing. She didn't let her children ride my back, either, at least, not in the air. It was one of her cardinal rules. Frankie and Camila, daredevils that they were, never stopped trying to find a loophole.

"No," Frankie called with a pout. He sat with his siblings at the kiddie table on the grass where their spills didn't warrant a clean-up, but close enough to the adults to hear and participate in the conversations. He'd been after his parents all summer to let him take some video me flying with him and his siblings all piled on my back. He wanted to post on noknok, the latest internet social media craze. Fortunately, his parents joined me in putting the kibosh on that.

I guess he thought that I would make an exception to his mom's rule in the interest of getting him the best grade. Rita and Jerry had recently introduced them to Harry Potter, and he'd been fascinated by the scene where Harry had ridden a hippogriff. No doubt he had visions of himself, arms around my neck and screaming with fright and delight as I launched myself from the playground and circled the schoolyard before taking off to skim one of the nearby lakes that gave the town its name.

Bendito. I'd squashed his chance at playground fame.

"I'd probably lose my license," I said, setting Father to chortling all over again.

Glad someone found it funny. When I first entered this world, one of the things I lost was the right to fly. Not the ability, mind you. The right. Apparently, the majesty of a dragon in flight was too much for the narrow-minded Mundanes to handle. I got blamed for a major accident on the highway, and humans have tried to shoot me out of the sky—even the military. But rather than taking the humans to task for their misbehavior, the authorities decided to ground me.

It had taken some fancy lawyering to come up with a solution. I had to have a pilot's license. Yes. To pilot myself. And any other flying creature crossing the Gap was going to have to face the same indignity. Guess who was getting the blame for that, too?

"Look on the bright side," Father had told me. "If you were your original size, you'd probably have to qualify for jumbo jets."

It was enough to drive a dragon to drink. Actually, it had. In the past two years in the Mundane, I'd lost most of my original Mundane friends, suffered innumerable indignities by civilians and authorities, not to mention the bad guys I went after, whether I got paid for it or not. Discovering the betrayal of some of my siblings led by my eldestkin, Durrehkeh, had put me on the edge, and having to get a license to do what comes as naturally as breathing had pushed me to regular visits to the Texaco, where five gallons of unleaded put a fuzzy coating over the sharp-edged world.

Better stop thinking about that. I'd promised Father I'd cut back. Time to change the subject. "Who's the Faerie nun helping Sister Mary Margaret?"

"That's Sister Grace," Anna Theresa answered from the kiddie table. "Nobody likes her."

"Anna Theresa Lucinda Costa!" Rita reproved.

"But, Mama, it's true." Jerry, Jr., the eldest, jumped to his sister's defense. "I overheard some teachers saying the only reason she's at the school is because both the Faerie and the Mundane bishops want it. People are scared of her."

Frankie added, "And Courtney was right. Sister Grace doesn't sing. Never. Even in Mass. She just grabs her big cross in a death grip and clenches her teeth. She looks mean."

Rita and Jerry, Sr., exchanged glances. So the parents knew? That made sense.

Jerry told his children, "I expect you to have a charitable heart and a Christian tongue when it comes to Sister Grace. You treat her with the same deference and respect you give all your teachers."

Father added, "She's had a difficult life. She needs your understanding, not your fear."

The children muttered, "Yes, sirs," but they didn't seem convinced.

Difficult life, huh? She wore the habit of a sister of Our Lady of Miracles, which meant she was a mage. Was that what scared people? Mundanes were a suspicious lot. A frowning mage who did not sing—and a religious...?

Of course, I also knew from experience that Mundanes saw what they looked for. It was almost a magic in itself. "People are usually scared of me at first," I said.

"Not me!" Jerry, Jr., said as he leaped from the table to grab his toddler sister before she toppled headfirst into the kiddie pool. He took his role as big brother very seriously. In fact, shortly after they'd moved into the house they'd inherited from Dona Elena, Junior approached me after Mass to hire me to protect his family from the "bad guys" that had followed them from Chicago. Tackling Mundane organized crime was somewhat more than I was ready for, but I did manage to garner an agreement to release Jerry from his obligations as a fence and secure his family a new start here in Los Lagos.

"You weren't afraid of me," I agreed, "but you did think I was scary."

"Dona Elena didn't think you were that scary, either," Father said, referring to the elderly parishioner who used to accuse me of eating her cats but who, in the end, willed me the warehouse I called home. She'd left Jerry's family her three-story Victorian, which turned out to be a fantastic home, now that they'd gotten rid of the cat smell.

"Must be a Costa thing," Father concluded.

"To Costa courage!" Jerry Senior raised his soda glass, and his children lifted their cups as well.

"And to Costa chili," I said, raising my bowl for seconds.

Chapter Two: Nonsense— or Nunsense?

Even 10 gallons of ethanol didn't take away the nightmares.

I was again hovering in the midst of a Faerie storm, dark clouds flashing with lightning, thunder rumbling around me. Another thunder—that of my kin—surrounded me on all sides, howling accusations I could not make out while I shouted for them to show themselves. Rain buffeted me from all sides—or perhaps it was the beating of over a hundred wings, I didn't know. Whenever I thought I was getting near enough to see one of my kin, they turned their tails to me and left. Soon, a handful remained, darting in and biting me, then spitting mouthfuls of my flesh into Hell.

I awoke roaring and scrabbling at the cement floor until my brain awoke enough to remind me I was safe and alone in the warehouse I was stuck calling "home." I squinted at the stacks of boxes full of dime-store dreck Señor Costa had collected in his eBay phase...probably about the time dementia was setting in, based on the quality and value of the trinkets I'd unpacked before deciding it was more valuable to leave the boxes unopened and imagine they held precious treasures. At the moment, with anguish and adrenaline coursing through my veins, I had the wild urge to let loose with my fire and torch it all.

I quelled it. Maybe it was greed. Maybe it was pride. But this was all I had in the Mundane world, and I wasn't going to sacrifice it in a vain attempt to appease the specters of memories nearly nine centuries old. Even if it would have helped my hangover.

I looked at my paws. I'd torn a claw. Great.

The rest of the morning went about as well. I started with the standard patrol of Territory—the area around my neighborhood that I'd claimed under my protection. That's how I'd discovered the palliative effects of fuel-grade petroleum. I'd stopped a robbery at the local Lickety-Split and the grateful store owner had offered me payment. Today, I declined his suggestion of a gallon or two in favor of a couple dozen just-expired eggs and some day-old hot dogs. Not the best breakfast in the world, but better than the rats I noshed on when things got rough and my belly got empty.

I chased off a couple of vandals spray-painting anti-Faerie slang, but they ducked into some occupied buildings, and I let them go rather than raise a fuss. I returned to examine the damage. Where did they learn this language? They'd chosen their canvas well. It was in direct line-of-site of the tenement mostly populated by the dryads they were insulting.

I wasn't going to let that stand. Finally, a good use for my fire today.

I'd burned through the worst of the words and was starting on the illustration when I heard the bwoop-bwoop of police sirens. Only one officer I knew could make a mechanical device sound both insolent and lazy. I steeled myself for the day to get bad again.

Out stepped Detective Sebastian Vialpando, who didn't even rate the phrase "Los Lagos' Finest" when used ironically. I swear the only reason he had a job was because he was Captain Santry's buddy. There were days I wished we'd stuck with Captain Beavers.

"Defacing private property? Even I didn't think you'd stoop this low. This some kind of weird instinct thing?"

I sneered back at him. "Re-facing, if you must know. It's a public service, not that I'd expect you to know anything about that."

"Watch it, dragon. I'm not afraid of you."

Of course, he wasn't. Vialpando was a jerk, but he wasn't a criminal. The only weapons I would use against him were my bad attitude and my wit—which, granted, was sharp as ever.

"It's funny how you have to remind yourself of that every time we meet. But I'm proud of you! You left your partner in the car this time."

He glanced back with surprise to see his car partner sitting in the passenger's seat, head bobbing and mouth moving as he listened to the latest upbeat earworm on the radio. Vialpando snorted in disgust. "It's that stupid song. Too catchy. Captain Santry banned it from the building, so I'm stuck hearing it on repeat in the car."

I did my most sarcastic version of a pitying pout. "Aw, can't you control your rookie?"

"Despite what you think of me, you worm-infested fewmet, I have a heart. We have an agreement about the choice of music. Later, he gets to listen to my Lazabel."

Mexican rage metal? Could he get more predictable? "I'd have had you pegged for Asesino."

He blinked. "You know....?"

"Don't get excited. We're not bonding. You know, the kids that did this were listening to that same song your partner's singing along to."

"Thanks. I'll add that to the description. 'Listens to obviously popular music like most Genzies.'"

"Okay, Boomer."

He curled his lip, then decided he'd bullied me enough for the day. "Get the owner to clean that up. We have laws against that kind of filth—and against the use of flamethrowers in city limits. Next time you forget that, I'll drag your tail in if I have to tie it to my car."

"Oh? You and the American Idol?" I jerked my nose toward his partner, who was still singing, oblivious to the world. Guess he didn't take this stop seriously, either.

Unfortunately, I'd overstepped. Vialpando flipped open his book and started scribbling. "Leave the kids to us. Captain Santry doesn't take kindly to thugs claiming part of our city as theirs—and that goes double for dragons who think they are doing a 'public service.'"

He ripped off the ticket, handed it to me, and gave the graffiti one last smirk.

He drove off, yelling at his rookie partner loudly enough to get past the music. I waited until all I heard was a dull rise and fall of his harping before looking at the ticket in my paw. Great. How was I going to pay this?

But as long as I was going to pay...

I turned around and blasted the wall. Let him try to drag my tail to jail. I was not having any dryads in my territory seeing what that Mundane in the sketch was doing with his chainsaw.

Needless to say, when I returned home, footsore and $140 poorer for my good deeds and for doing what a dragon is made to do, I was not in the mood for company, especially the problematic mage-sister who scared fourth graders. But she was sitting on my front step, praying the rosary. Next to her lay a folder under a large rock. She must have put it there but at an arm's distance. Odd.

Rif and Raf, the mongrels I'd picked up to watch my property while I was out watching others, sat flanking her protectively. That was odd, too. They usually had a healthy suspicion of strangers. Well, "healthy," for my purposes. More than one vagabond had lost a bit of their pants to my pets' teeth. It spared me from doing it myself.

She looked up as I approached. Her eyes were blue like Faerie Medsea. It made me homesick. I jerked my chin toward the folder. "Thank you notes from the kids or complaints from the parents?" The way my day was going, I expected the latter.

"Are you available for hire?" she replied instead.

Now, my curiosity was piqued. Plus, I needed the money. I invited her in. I didn't bother leading her down the long corridor of boxes to my desk. That was for clients I wanted to make work for my services. Instead, we took a right into the small kitchen that once must have been a break room, though what any human was taking a break from here was a mystery I might never solve. My "lair" was a long warehouse with a small public office and the break room as you entered, while through the dividing doors, there was a main section stuffed with boxes and metal shelves and a partial second story that held a supervisor's office. There was even a bathroom and a shower—another mystery, and both useless to me. I wondered if sometimes Señor Costa hadn't used this as his getaway from his Señora. Dona Elena was a feisty old bat right up to the end of her life.

I used my 270-degree vision to get a more complete look at Sister Grace than I had while distracted by children. She was average for a Faerie human, five-two, maybe 140 pounds. A good amount of muscle, but enough fat to tell me she ate well and had probably been enjoying Mundane cuisine for at least a year. I felt a pang of envy. Wish I had enough food to fatten myself up. Her face looked pleasant enough, except that it was pinched with stress. All of her muscles were tight. I could feel waves to tension flowing off her.

That wasn't what caught my attention the most, however. It was the magic flowing around her, hesitant and held at bay. Most mages, most Magicals, took in at least a small wisp of magic. It was so commonplace, I didn't notice. Grace was at once attracting magic and pushing it away, and the effect struck my senses like air with too much static.

I dumped my ticket in a drawer to deal with later. I offered her some tea, which she declined, and a seat, which she accepted, sitting forward as if she'd need to spring up at any moment. Clearly, a nun on the edge, literally and figuratively. She pushed the folder across the table at me. I flipped it open.

"Music? You know dragons don't sing."

"I'm not asking you to sing. I'm asking you to look at it closely. What do you see?"

I flipped through the pages. It was the words and notes for that awful earworm that had been hounding me all day. The title proudly declared it "Mishmash" by a band called Acoustic Blenda. I grimaced.

"So, you do see it!" she said triumphantly.

"See what?"

"Look again. Look at it as a dragon of the Inquisition. There is evil there."

"Like a spell?" If so, no wonder she was keeping it at arm's distance. I looked again, more carefully. Meanwhile, she sat perched on the edge of the cheap plastic chair, arms in her lap, face placid. It was a ruse. I could feel the tension in her muscles and the swirling of magical energies around her. I got the feeling she'd gladly set fire to this particular sheet of music, if only she could guarantee that would erase all traces of it from the Mundane universe. I wondered if she would turn on me if I gave her an answer she didn't want to hear. Religious or not, she seemed to be barely hanging on to whatever control she had on her temper and her magics.

She couldn't kill me, of course, but I had no doubt she could severely inconvenience me for a few decades.

But all I saw was a bunch of random noises put to music.

"I'm sorry, Sister. They're just nonsense sounds. Mishmash. Just like the name promises."

I braced myself, but instead of the attack I half-expected, she asked me, as if I were an idiot, "Have you even heard this song?"

I shrugged. It'd only been hounding me all day. "It's Top Ten, and I have very good hearing. It's not like I can avoid it."

"Have you really listened to it? Or have you let it grip your brain and strangle your ability to think like it has most of the population?"

Religious or not, no one insults me in my lair. I got enough of that everywhere else. I snarled with all my teeth. Instead of backing down, she stood and slammed her hand on the table. "Look again, dragon! It has syntax! It is a language. And I'm almost certain it is Faerie. Wisdom of the Ages. Experience of Eternity—isn't that what your ad says?"

That hurt worse than the proverbial ruler across the knuckles.

I didn't have to stand to loom over her. I just stretched my neck until we were snout to nose. "Listen, Sister: I may have had an encyclopedic knowledge of languages in the past, but thanks to Saint George—"

She flung her head dismissively. "I know. Saint George took away all your dragon abilities, and you have to earn them back through serving God and His creatures. And do you try?"

"I've been trying for 858 years, five months, three weeks, and two days. I have given up all my possessions, humbled myself before lesser creatures, fought in two Great Wars for the side of Good—"

She cut me off. "Have you prayed a novena?"

"A novena?" I blinked, my prepared rant short-circuited by her simple question.

"Aye, a novena! A nine-day series of intercessory prayers."

"I know what a novena is! Why would I bother?"

"To regain what you've lost, you silly dragon!"

Surprise made me pull back. Pray my abilities back? Maybe I was an idiot. Not that anyone had ever mentioned the possibility of praying to get back my powers, so how was I to know?

"Would that actually work?" I asked.

She rubbed her eyes with one hand while the other clutched her cross. Was she asking for patience, strength, or maybe the answer to my question? I gave her time to collect herself.

Finally, she said, "Maybe not a return of knowledge for its own sake, but if the need is great..." She shrugged.

Was the need great? She seemed to think so. I looked at the sheet music again. Nonsense sounds.

Then again, I was never much of a linguist, that I remembered, anyway. Part of what I lost in my battle with St. George was my memories—and when you were created on the Eighth Day, that's a lot to lose. I wondered if any of my kin had especially enjoyed languages, but then I dismissed the thought. They were gone, and I was alone. No sense pushing on a bruise.

I asked, "Have you talked to anyone else about this—the music, I mean? There are linguists in the Faerie and the Mundane."

"I have," she sat back down. "They think I'm—they don't see anything either. But I know it's there and it's sinister and we have to do something before..."

She shrugged. She clenched and relaxed her fists.

"Before it gets too popular?" I suggested, then snorted. "It's too late for that, Sister. Besides, even if either of us had any real influence, this is the Mundane. Specifically, the United States of

America. They can't even master censorship on social media."

"Then we have to be ready to deal with what happens," she said, and it didn't take dragon senses to know the thought terrified her.

Two days later, I still didn't have any leads on the song, so I did what any modern dragon in the Mundane would do. I brought it up to my online DnD group during our monthly game.

Linda made a disgusted face. "I hate that song. Why are you so interested? Um, I roll 15 Perception. Do I hear anything?"

"You hear a muffled something from outside the cave, but you can't tell if it's footsteps or snow falling from the trees. Remember, last time we met, you had run into the cave because of a minor avalanche," Ray, our dungeon master said.

Our group used to play every week, but now, my human friends had scattered across the country—and, in Samwise's case, into Faerie. We now met once every second Tuesday online. I did enjoy the internet. Sam still had problems, as the Interdimensional internet was choppy at best, but since it was his job to get it running, he got the best connection in that world.

Sam asked, "Can I tell? I roll...17. I haven't heard it—the song, that is."

Ray answered. "Count yourself lucky, then. I made the mistake of downloading the album. Aside from this one song, they are awful. Worse than me. Worse than me before Titania gave me gifted fingers."

We all winced. Ray liked to cosplay a bard, but before our adventure in Faerie, had only known three chords. He had a modicum of talent and a reasonable voice, but nothing good enough for even community theater or the local Ren Fest. Titania, Queen of the Summer Court of Fairies, had given him the ability to remember any song he practiced at, which meant he could be reasonably entertaining at parties (as a guest) or not get booed off the stage during Amateur Nights.

He continued, "Yeah, I don't get the appeal. Maybe it's a GenZ thing? Anyway, Sam, you also hear muffled sounds."

Sam said he turned toward the sound.

Meanwhile, Linda continued our out-of-character conversation. "It's not that. The song is just creepy. I have this visceral reaction. I snap off the radio every time it comes on."

Owen retorted, "You snap off the radio every time you think a commercial is going to repeat a phone number or website three times."

Instead of taking offense, she jumped on his comment with enthusiasm. "Exactly! It's the same thing. It's like it's trying to get in my head."

While Owen countered that that was what a good song was meant to do, Father Rich reminded everyone that he had Mass and a wedding to perform tomorrow and needed to log off on-time, so Ray made us roll for initiative.

Nonetheless, after we'd killed the owlbear and made camp in the cave and everyone else logged off, Father remained to talk to me. "Who wants you to investigate the song?"

"Sorry. I'm getting paid. Detective-client confidentiality."

"I thought I was your Archibald."

Father had gotten me started in the detective business when he asked me to help him prove the innocence of a young migrant worker accused of murder. At the time, I was new to the Mundane and limited in what I could do in public, and he'd offered to play Archibald to my Nero, referring to the famous house-bound detective. That was three years and a dozen cases ago.

"You promised your sister, the Sister, no more adventures. Besides, you're busy with the school, now, too. When are they going to bring another priest to the parish?"

My attempt to distract him failed. "I only know one other person who reacts as badly as Linda to that song."

I snorted. "You're not asking around enough. Lots of people hate that song."

"I didn't say, 'hate.' I said who had an adverse reaction." When I didn't rise to his bait, he sighed. "Look, I'm glad you're getting paid, but be careful. There's stuff about Sister Grace you don't know. Stuff I'm not comfortable sharing. And I know you never said, 'Sister Grace,' but just in case, if... Let me know if you do need help, and how the case progresses."

We logged off, and I sat back on my haunches, annoyed. It was starting to look like getting to understand my client was going to be at least as important as uncovering the mystery of this song. If there was a mystery. I still hadn't decided.

At least I was getting paid.

But as I drifted off to sleep, the hidden context of Father's words made themselves known to me, along with another thought. What if the only problem with the song was what was in Sister Grace's head? I didn't like to use the word 'crazy' when referring to a religious, but if she was, and this was some kind of delusion... Was it morally okay to take her money?

I sighed, thinking about the computer I'd just shut down. Bills were coming due. Electricity was becoming as important to me as my fire. I had to figure her out, but in the meantime, money was money. If I had to, I'd pay her back later, somehow.

Chapter Three: Nunplussed

Sister Grace came over the next day to see what her money was getting her and to decide if she wanted to pay more. The way she scowled at the folder, two-inches thick with printed papers and my handwritten analysis, I was thinking my previous night's worries were for naught.

"I dinna ask for a dissertation," she said, annoyance bringing out her Irish accent.

I was feeling rather Ire-ish, myself. "You asked me to analyze the song. Since I didn't have any insights from my wisdom of the ages, I did it the hard way.

"You said it had syntax. It does—in the way the language twin babies babble at each other might have syntax. Nothing that corresponds to a civilized use of language. At least, that's how Doctor Raymond at CSU-Los Lagos put it."

She flipped through the pages. "You asked a Mundane?"

"I asked a university professor. You paid me to do a job, and I'm nothing if not thorough. The sounds, either singly or in groups, don't correspond to any known language, and the repetition seems merely for the sake of the music. So, dead end on the linguistics.

"You're worried it's evil. I looked up the band. Acoustic Blenda is a pop band aimed at tweens and teens. Hardly the music genre of Satan." I paused there, remembering one particularly hellish car ride where Anna Theresa insisted on playing "What Does the Fox Say" on a loop. "But I could be wrong on that. Nonetheless, the four members of the band are clean: no criminal record, no rumors of drug use or cultish behavior. About the edgiest thing any of them have done is the lead singer got a tattoo after being inspired to write the song."

I flipped to the picture I'd pulled from the band's website. Connor Beck, the lead singer, had his sleeve rolled up to show off his monster tattoo. I wondered if he was drunk when he asked for it, or if the artist was just that bad. Or maybe the artist was drunk. Either way, it was a sloppy rendition of a tentacled creature with fangs. Too many tentacles and too many fangs, all in the wrong places. It was as if he'd said, "sort of octopus and Cthulhu and that sand trap thing from Star Wars" and the artist just rolled with it. Yet Beck was grinning like a he'd won the Lottery of Skin Art.

"It's no creature I can find in the Grimoire or my own memory," I told Sister Grace. "I even checked the DnD Monster Manual."

"The what?"

I shrugged. "Never mind. The point is, this isn't any known monster or demon in reality or fiction—although, I know, demons can take any form they feel like, and Mundanes have plenty of imagination. But honestly, look at it. Would any self-respecting demon voluntarily take that form?"

She looked again and shrugged. "It is pretty nonsensical."

"Just like the song. Chances of demonic influence: low. I'm sorry, Sister. I'm not finding anything to corroborate your suspicions."

"Well, keep at it," she said, and before I could protest that she was wasting her money and my time, she added, "we have six more days, after all."

"Six more days?" Was there a deadline I didn't know about?

She looked as surprised at my question as I was at her statement. Then her eyes narrowed. "For the novena? You have been praying, have ye not?"

She was getting that Joan of Arc expression. I'd gone head-to-head with that saint more than once, but never about a novena. "No. I didn't realize it was required."

"All this time spent on research, but you couldn't spend twenty minutes in prayer?"

I shrugged. "Guess I didn't believe it'd help?"

She crossed her arms and glared. "'Did not believe,'" she repeated. "Do ye not believe in me, or in yourself? Or is faith the issue in general?"

"Listen, Sister," I growled. "Don't think about lecturing me on faith. I am an Eighth Day Creation. I was made to inspire mortals to prayer. Now, I live in squalor among mortals, and I don't have the ability to pray the way my kind was meant to pray. I've spent 858 years under the authority of the Faerie mortal's Church. I have obeyed its laws. I have prayed its prayers."

"Have ye? Like you have the novena I suggested?"

I continued more loudly atop her words. "I have fought under its command to defend mortal lives that are a gnat's span compared to mine!"

"Aye, I know your deeds," she snarled back. "I'm very aware of how you saved all Faerie in the last war."

Yet, no "thank you" passed her lips. "And are you aware the price I paid? The suffering I endured as a result?"

Then she did something I would not have expected from a nun, especially one from a Faerie who knew our history and the power commanded by the forces of evil there. She snorted and shook her head.

No one dismisses my pain in my lair. "I think we're done. Good afternoon to you, Sister Grace," I managed to say with cold politeness. She may not respect me, but I'd at least try to respect her.

She blinked, as if surprised. When my expression didn't change, she shrugged, but pulled out three Franklins from her pocket and set them on the table. Ouch. She knew my language.

"I want you to keep working. You may not believe, but I do. There's something here, and we will find it."

I wanted to laugh at her the way she'd laughed at me. I wanted to tell her she was wasting my time and that this was a crazy quest. But I didn't. Maybe it was the money reminding me I had bills. More likely, it was the way the nebulous tendrils of magic had gathered around her, like a charge waiting for the spell to be cast, yet she didn't embrace it like most mages do. In fact, she seemed to put an effort into holding it away from her.

When she said she believed, was it in herself, in me, or faith in general?

"Fine," I said, "on one condition. Tell me why you are so interested in music when you won't sing."

Her hand rested on the table. For a moment, I thought she'd snatch my advance away rather than answer the question. Finally, she said in a voice so low, if I hadn't had superior hearing, I'd have missed it: "You're not the only one who was hurt in the Great War."

Abruptly, she gathered the materials, promising to study them herself, and I escorted her to the door. She paused before stepping across the threshold and turned to me. "About the novena."

"What about it?"

She sighed. A defeated, heart-wrenching, guilt-inducing sigh of disappointment and resignation. "Vurnerrah, I've been praying for you. And I want you to pray. A novena. For this. For me. Consider it part of what I'm paying you for and start tonight."

"I will," I promised, thoroughly chagrined. That doesn't happen often to me. I wonder if she was getting help from Above. St. Joan always knew how to put me in my place, though she was more direct about it. Maybe St. Hildegard? Yeah, she'd be interested in music and would probably hate this song as much as Sister Grace does. I could pray a novena to her—though St. Jude was the better choice. He was patron saint of lost causes, after all, and I didn't see any way I was going to win.

In the end, I chose a purely Faerie saint: St. Ailyftmisonnguphiindlowd, patron saint of minstrels and madness. St. Ailyft for short, as short was often needed when dealing with elvish names. Seemed appropriate to the situation. Bards had been known to call on his protection after they'd annoyed a dragon one too many times. Usually, it worked. Regardless, the irony of a dragon calling on St. Ailyft amused me, and Sister Grace had asked me to pray for her, too.

Wouldn't you know? The next morning, I woke up with an idea for another lead. If no one but Sister Grace saw something wrong with this nonsense song, then what was it about her that made her see something sinister? Time to investigate my employer.

Father Rich had made it clear that he was not going to tell me anything about her—not anything I'd consider useful to my situation, at any rate—so I decided to go to the one person he might talk to. I called his sister, Sister Bernadette.

"Vern! This is a surprise!" she said, then her voice grew suspicious. "Is Ricky all right?"

There was a reason I didn't call her often. Before she launched into follow-ups, I said, "I haven't gotten him shot at or stabbed or the target of any malicious spells, and he's sticking to his diet. Mostly. I'm calling because I was wondering if you knew anything about the new religious sister in the parish, Sister Grace McCarthy. Has he mentioned her?"

There was a pause, then she said, "That is one thing I like about you, Vern. No pretense."

"Was that sarcasm? How very un-Christian and in character."

She laughed. "Yes, he's mentioned her. Why aren't you asking him?"

"I did. I want your impression. It's for an investigation."

She tsked with annoyance. "You can reassure whatever parent hired you that they are worrying needlessly. She doesn't even use her abilities anymore. She's all right, and even if she weren't, Rick has a good handle on the situation. He won't let her hurt anyone. Okay?"

Her four sentences had sparked about a dozen questions, but I knew that tone of voice. I wouldn't get more from her today. "Thanks. That does help. Still enjoying Houston?"

She hummed assent. "The work, yes, and the weather. But I miss the mountains."

We made some small talk, mostly because we both felt it was expected. I mentioned the song, but if she'd heard it, it hadn't made an impression. Apparently, it wasn't the overplayed earworm it was in Colorado, but she did admit she mostly listened to country, Latin, and zydeco lately.

"Zydeco is oddly popular in Houston," she told me. Since it was a uniquely Mundane music genre, I didn't know much about it, and she promised to send me some links to expand my musical horizons. Before we hung up, I asked her not to mention this call to Father, and she reluctantly agreed.

"Though if parents are spreading bad blood, he should know," she chided me, and I in turn promised to let him know if I suspected trouble.

Talking to random parents would indeed "spread bad blood" as Sister B put it, and the only parents I personally knew were the Costas, who had already proven themselves as closed-mouthed as Father. So, I went to the next best source of rumors. Fortunately, I'd already agreed to babysit the Costa kids. The things I'll do for Rosa's chili.

I'd originally fallen into watching the kids because Jerry and Rosa had desperately needed a break and couldn't find a responsible teen willing to ride herd on four active children under 11 in a house that stank of cats. Besides which, the thugs that were intimidating Jerry were still at large; neither Rita nor Jerry was going to leave their kids without protection. Dragons are not nurturers by nature, but we'd bonded at Dona Elena's funeral—it turned out that dragon purrs, a prehensile tail, and the occasional show of teeth were enough to keep everyone in line and reasonably content while Mom and Dad had a date night. Over the years, it had grown into a regular thing, which helped me now because I didn't need a pretense to get the kids alone.

As it turned out, I didn't need a pretense to get them talking about Sister Grace, either. All it took was pizza and to ask how school went that week.

"Sister Grace and Missus Orien got into a fight in the office today," Jerry, Jr. reported with some glee as he pulled the paper plates out of the pantry. Maria carried a roll of paper towels into the living room. Anna Theresa was working the remote to pick the movie, and Frankie and Camila had spread a blanket in front of the TV so they could sit and eat while they watched. Jerry had had to replace the carpet and part of the floor to get rid of the cat smell, and Rita was adamant that her new carpet not get food stains. "I was picking up tests for Mister Pachenko, and I heard them yelling in the principal's office."

"Yelling, really?" I asked as I prepped a bottle for the baby. Baby Gloria was chewing on one of my spikes. There was nothing glorious about the amount of drool she generated. Wisdom of the Ages, Knowledge of Eternity, and I was a teething toy. "What would two teachers be yelling to the principal about?"

"That song, what else? Misses O said she was going to teach it to us, and Sister Grace got really mad. She said Missus O must not be a good teacher if she can't teach us anything better than that."

"Ouch!" I said to keep Jerry talking.

"I know, right? But I think Missus O started it. She called Sister Grace paranoid."

"What's 'parinoid'?" Camila asked.

"Paranoid. P A R A N O I D," I spelled, then translated to Spanish and elvish because Francisco picked up language like sponge, and if I had to be a babysitter, I was going to be the best ever. "It means you think someone's after you or that something bad is going to happen to you. But just because you're paranoid…"

"Doesn't mean it's not true," the older two chorused. I'd taught them that, and it had come in handy when Marone's thugs tried to nab them to use as bargaining chips to get Jerry to return to Chicago. The mob boss hadn't taken lightly to his best fence going straight.

Anna Theresa handed out sippy cups of sparkling water—the only drink allowed on the carpet. "Missus O is nice, and I like that song. It's fun. Sister Grace is just mean."

"I like her!" Francisco protested. "She doesn't let Randy get away with anything. Addison, either."

"Addison is nice," Anna retorted.

"She's a teacher's pet," Frankie said.

"Well, so am I!"

"Because you're smart," Frankie told his sister. "Addison is a suck up. That's what Randy says. Vern, what's a suck up?"

I spelled it, translated it, then said, "Someone who flatters other people or pretends to be extra nice so that the other person will like them best. But it's not meant to be a compliment."

"Yeah, I knew that much," Francisco said. "That's why I don't say that around Mom and Dad. Still, it fits."

"You're just jealous because she's popular and the teachers all like her."

"Suck up!" Maria sang and was promptly shushed by her siblings. Undeterred, she started to march around the blanket chanting "suck up" and trying to spell it. Meanwhile, Frankie was prancing and posing as he mocked his classmate.

"Look at me! I'm Addison Lukas! I'm gorgeous and I'm the best singer and I'll be a noknok star someday..."

"Stop it!" Anna yelled. "That's mean."

"I make all the teachers love me because I'm a suck up..."

Maria chanted, "Suck up! S U K—UP—P..."

"Vern!" Anna stomped her foot.

This is what my life has been reduced to—elementary school politics. I needed to get everyone back on the topic I was interested in. "It didn't look to me like Addison was trying to suck up to Sister Grace much."

"Addison doesn't like her, either," Anna Theresa reported. "She said her daddy said Sister Grace killed someone with her magic and that she should still be locked away, not teaching school."

"Still be locked away?" I pounced on the clue like one of the many cats that had once prowled this room.

"That's stupid," Jerry told his sister. "They wouldn't let a crazy person be a teacher."

"She's not a teacher. She's a helper. And the only reason she's there is because Bishop Thomas wants to be good friends with the Faerie bishop."

"Suck up! S K P U V W X..."

"That's stupid! Addison just doesn't like her because Sister Grace won't fall for her goody-two-shoes act."

"Suck up," Maria chanted. "Two shoes. One shoe, two shoe, red shoe, suck shoes…"

"Maria Magdalena Costa, stop it!" Anna shouted. Maria's lip started to pout and quiver, but Anna Theresa interested me more. She had started to shake, and tears were welling in her eyes.

With a gesture, I directed Jerry to distract his littler sister and got my face to Anna's eye level. "Are you scared of Sister Grace?"

She sniffled and wrapped her arms around herself in a hug. "It's not just Addison, you know. Jackson's dad works night shifts at a half-way house for crazy people, and he said Sister Grace lives there. He said he hears her casting spells in her room. Jackson's mom wants to take him out of school and everything. Other kids have heard things from their parents. They say she was crazy and put spells on people and that's why they sent her here to the Mundane where she couldn't use magic. But that's stupid. People can use magic here."

"You're right," I told her but in my calmest and most reassuring voice. "But I know Bishop Aiden. He would never send someone dangerous to the Mundane, and especially not to a school full of innocent children. There has to be a reason she's here, and I'm going to try to find out, okay? In the meantime, you don't need to be afraid."

She shrugged and refused to meet my eyes.

Fortunately, the doorbell rang just then, and the mood brightened as Jerry and Frankie paid the delivery man and brought in fragrant, hot pizza. Everyone sat on the blanket with their plates and drinks. I got Gloria settled in the crook of my arm with her bottle while I passed out slices—prehensile tail, remember—and we settled down to watch a movie about an umbrella-carrying nanny.

"You're sure Sister Grace is okay?" Anna asked me as on the screen, the father sang about order in his house.

"I'm certain she has no intention of hurting any of you. I think she's more likely to hurt someone else to protect you," I said. "Just like I would."

"Okay, then." She turned her attention to the show and her second slice.

When Mary Poppins declared herself "Practically perfect in every way," Jerry leaned against my flank.

"Not as perfect as you, Vern," he said.

"Suck up!" Maria said.

Chapter Four: Nun of Mystery

Kids make great informants. Grace did not teach music, but Faerie Studies. They didn't know the name of the "halfway house," but they did know Jackson's dad's first and last name. ("Because he never calls him Dad," Frankie sneered). Sister Grace had lived in Mundane almost since the Gap stabilized and people could travel through, but somewhere back East, maybe Washington DC, because Frankie said she talked about the Smithsonian and the Catholic University of America a lot and that she'd told them she'd taken a sabbatical to study Mundane liturgical music.

Frankie obviously adored the Faerie nun, and I had to break up two fights between him and her sister before their parents got home. I flew home thanking God that dragons don't reproduce.

I spent the rest of the evening and part of the morning doing a background search. She had done research at the Catholic University, but that was almost six months after she'd arrived. A year studying music, but not doing anything with her newfound knowledge; then moving here to teach Faerie history to a bunch of kids...

About 2 a.m., I went for a midnight flight and sniffed around until I located Grace's scent and noted the address. As I veered off, I heard her cry out in her sleep, not much more than a mumble to her housemates, but clear enough to me. She was speaking in Faerie Gaelic. Probably why Jackson's dad thought she was casting spells. Typical Mundane ignorance. One mystery solved, I started home again, when I heard, *Let me go. Don't let them touch me! God, where are you?*

I returned, hovered, and listened to her argue with the captors in her dream: *No! I will not serve you. My magic is God's alone. Stop it! I will not sing for you! God, please!*

Who was she talking to? Was it a real threat from her past, a phantom stirred up by her sub-conscious—or something real and new?

I stayed outside her window until her cries became moans and subsided.

Grace lived in a three-story apartment complex—22 apartments total. I didn't find much about it online, so I hung out on the roof behind the air vent where no one casually looking up would see me loitering and call the police to report a dragon lurking in their neighborhood. It happened more often than you'd think. I wondered if Mundanes would ever get used to me. Then, I listened. I heard alarms go off, people making breakfasts, opening bottles of pills. Lots of bottles of pills. Not the heavy megavitamin kind.

A car pulled up, and a woman in professional dress walked in. Not long after that came the sounds of discussion, a group of people talking about their week. It was a guided discussion, led, I guessed, by the woman in the beige pantsuit I'd seen enter.

"And what about you, Sister Grace?" I heard the woman say. "Anything interesting happen to you this week?"

Grace spent the next few minutes entertaining them with the antics of the children of St. Scholastica. She had a talent for storytelling. There were no lies, I'm sure; but there was more than one kind of blarney. She didn't divulge anything useful, neither for me nor for the counselor leading the group discussion. She didn't mention her nightmare, the fight with the music teacher, or her visits to me. That was interesting.

When her turn was done, they moved on to some guy complaining about his job at Burger Barn. As he griped about no one telling him anything, I spread my wings and left. If he thought he didn't get enough information to do his job, he should try a week as me.

"Bless me, Father, for I have sinned. It's been three days since my last confession. I made the Los Despredatores' newest recruit pee his pants. Then I laughed, because it really was kind of funny..."

Across from me, Bishop Aiden listened attentively and tried not to grin. Los Despredatores was the local gang in my area, and we had an ongoing minor war. Most of the time, I tried to "scare them straight," as my friend Sheriff Bert likes to say. Lately, it's become a kind of rite of passage; if the new recruit can take the heat of the resident dragon, he was in. Not a bad initiation ceremony as far as gangs went since they didn't kill anyone, and I didn't kill them. But the Church had decided that dragons purposely making humans void their bladders was a Bad Thing, so I confessed it on an all-too regular basis. Today, however, it was just the warmup. I had something else I needed to get off my soul before I met again with Sister Grace. But I also needed answers before I decided whether I wanted to go on meeting with Sister Grace.

Hence, my traveling to Faerie to give my confession to him rather than Fr. Rich.

"...and I eavesdropped. And cyberstalked someone. Professionally, sort of. It's part of a case."

"Sort of?" the bishop spoke archly with both tone and raised brow.

I shrugged and agreed, "Sort of."

The bishop absolved me and gave me my penance. Then he rang for a page, who came in bearing refreshment—tea and little sandwiches for him, a raw chicken doused in a simmering sauce for me. I also had tea, but in a platter on the floor. Around humans in the Mundane, I do my best to fit in, which means having proper table matters, but here in Faerie, I could relax and eat as a dragon is meant to eat. Sort of.

At my side were several mailing tubes holding copies of the song.

My last few days had not turned up much. Jackson's dad did indeed work in Grace's building, as the janitor. The apartments Grace lived in were indeed for those "transitioning back into society" after some kind of breakdown...and the fact that Grace never mentioned the music or her nightmares in any of her sessions meant she wasn't fully cooperating with the process. And her therapist knew it.

Grace was not on social media, but a few of the other residents were, including a chatty female who was "sharing her process" on her blog. In between self-indulgent diatribes about her struggle to love herself, she mentioned other housemates...including the Faerie nun who "encourages us to embrace joy but doesn't seem to have much herself."

When I start feeling bad about my body, I like to watch Shrek. *It's such a message of hope that even at our ugliest, there's someone who can love us. So a couple of us were in the common room, and Sister Grace came in and sat with us. I don't think I'd ever seen her laugh so much. She has a pretty, musical laugh, and it made us all want to laugh even more.*

But then we came to the scene where Fiona is singing with the bird. You know, the iconic Snow White scene but where Fiona makes the bird sing so high and long it explodes? Well, we were all laughing, and Sister Grace just stands up and, and flees.

I saw the look on her face before she left. It wasn't judgmental. It was *horrified,* like she was looking into the depths of Hell itself.

I'm not sure I can watch Shrek *the same way again.*

That blog entry should have convinced me that this whole song obsession was in her head. Instead, it just made me want to look harder. But I still didn't find anything in the song. Even worse, I heard Grace chiding me. "Wisdom of the Ages, Experience of Eternity? Isn't that what your website says?"

It did, but the truth was, it was advertising. My wisdom was blunted after my encounter with St. George, and my experience limited to my life after that battle.

Which was when I realized that just because I didn't find any answers in my own past or in the wisdom of the internet, did not mean I might not find it elsewhere in Faerie. Hence, the second reason for my visit—and Confession. Bishop Aiden always feels more amenable after serving one of his flock. Plus, being the bishop of the diocese on the Faerie side of the Gap, he liked knowing what was going on in the Mundane.

So we talked a little about the gang in my territory, and how I was at turns smacking them down when they got too destructive and trying to form a relationship with them to make them better people. He wasn't sure how my pouncing on them and drooling into their faces was going to further that, but he was willing to trust me. At least, I could report that their latest recruit wanted nothing more to do with the gang—or any other gang in the area. He seemed to think there was a "cool factor" to membership. His soggy seat disabused him of that idea.

Now, Bishop Aiden allowed himself the smile he'd scrupulously suppressed while hearing my confession. But soon enough, his gaze turned inquisitive, and he nodded toward the tubes at my side. "I feel your visit was not fully social nor spiritual."

"I need some things delivered and a reply back as quickly as possible."

He leaned over and picked up one of the messages, the one addressed to the monastery in Alexandria. He pursed his lips. "This is the case you are working on?"

I nodded.

"More 'cyberstalking, sort of'?"

"No. This is directly part of the case. Research I'm being paid for, but not enough to pay for a quick, direct delivery."

"I see. And so, you have come to me." He set the scroll down next to his scone and dainty sandwiches. "And what have you discerned about your client, Sister Grace?"

"What do you mean?" I hedged.

He indicated the scrolls. "These hold, I assume, the music and lyrics to the song she is so suspicious of. You have not asked her for more money to arrange delivery but come asking a favor of me. Or are you wanting more than the use of my delivery mages?"

I always did appreciate how savvy Bishop Aiden was. It saved me a lot of time explaining things. "Why did you send her to the Mundane?"

His face was as bland as when he heard my Confession. "But I did not send her. Her order did."

"Our Lady of Miracles? I recognized the habit. A religious order of mages, but Grace doesn't do magic. In fact, she seems afraid of it. Can you explain that?"

"You've not answered my question. Do you believe her about the music?" the bishop asked.

I shrugged. "She's a client."

He tried again. "And yet you have cyber-stalked and eavesdropped on her. Do you trust her?"

My annoyance spiked. I'd come to get answers, not to get interrogated. Once again, I was being reminded that even in my own world, I was not my own dragon.

"Each day she pays me," I replied.

He sighed. "The Mundane world has changed you, Vern."

I barked out a laugh. "Did you like me better when I was risking my skin battling the forces of evil for you mortals? Just because I can't die doesn't mean I can't be hurt. The Despredatores are child's play compared to what I've put up with in the defense of all that is good and holy on Faerie."

"I have read the chronicles. I know all that you did," he spoke softly. "And not just for us mortals."

"That's right. I fought for us all, even my own kind after they abandoned me—and what have I gotten in return? I'm stuck on the other side of the Gap. I live in a lousy lair which I pay for with a lousy job, but at least I'm the one who decides what lousy tasks I take on."

"I understand," he said softly, and I believed he did. I also believed that he wouldn't hesitate to conscript me if need be.

He continued. "And yet, you still do not answer my question. Let me ask differently: since you have a choice, do you continue with this lousy task from Sister Grace for the money?" He refilled my drinking dish, then his cup.

"No." My answer surprised me. True, I wanted the money, and the things it brought me. But if I had to, I could hustle other jobs. I could always use my grocery money for the internet bill and get by on rats. Not my favorite cuisine, but I've done it rather than take on a job I didn't want.

"Why then?"

I had to think about that. I finished my bowl of tea and let the bishop's page refill it. When he'd left, I said, "She interests me."

He smiled, that kind of proud, satisfied smile humans get when something goes their way. I felt like I'd passed some sort of test. I also felt like I wouldn't get any straight answers from him today.

He picked up the rest of the scrolls. "I'd like her to go on interesting you, Vern. Even after this case is done. She is a very valued member of her order, and of my flock. And I believe the two of you may have more in common than you know.

There may be ways you can help her, even beyond this assignment."

"Help her with what?"

"You will have to discover that for yourself, as well as how she may be of benefit to you." He set down the scroll and picked up the bell next to the teapot. In a moment, his page had appeared, with the bishop's secretary, Father Vic, close behind. "Patrick, see that this is delivered by fastest means to the St. Athanasius Scriptorium in Alexandria."

I pointed to the others at my side. "And these. The recipients are on the label."

At the secretary's bidding, the boy gathered the scrolls and hurried off. Once the door closed, Father Vic spoke.

"I'm afraid there's been a development in Los Lagos. Sister Grace McCarthy is being taken into custody. They say she placed a curse on a child."

Chapter Five: Innuncent Until Proven Guilty

Bailing out nuns was not something a bishop did, "part of his flock" or not. So while he had word sent to her order, he tasked me to go find out what was going on, and if needed, post whatever funds were necessary to secure her freedom and then escort her home.

I did not have a good relationship with the Los Lagos police department. My first encounter had been with Police Chief Beavers, who liked to play at being my greatest fan while he stabbed me in the back in his attempt to make sure everyone felt comfortable having a dragon in town. His efforts landed me in the zoo. In the end, I uncovered evidence that got him implicated in a case of industrial espionage as well as accessory to murder. I didn't get to eat him, but I did get him run out of office and behind bars. Sweet enough revenge.

Or it would have been if the city hadn't replaced him with one Captain Michael Santry from L.A., a lawful-good boy scout as uptight as his haircut. The council brought him in because he had a reputation for honesty. He was honest all right: honestly suspicious of all magic and Faerie, and particularly of a certain sincere dragon sent by God to the Mundane to do Good. He might not have tricked me into wearing a monitoring anklet or tossed me in the zoo, but he has hauled me into an interrogation room and once threatened to shoot me.

Needless to say, I did not have a good feeling about a mage being subjected to the not-so-tender mercies of the city's newest chief of police, so when I crossed the Gap and felt the confused and tormented gathering of magical energies in the direction of the police department, I launched myself into the air and put on as much speed as I could. I had no idea what Sister Grace could do with magic—or what magic would do with Sister Grace—but it terrified her. That was enough to worry me.

By the time I got there, the magic was still close, but somehow calmer. I rarely assigned emotion to magic, any more than one might normally assign emotion to the weather. Nonetheless, if I'd still felt terror in the magic, I'd have busted straight in. As it was, I felt comfortable enough to go in the front door and ask the desk sergeant.

Just my luck, it was Officer Tracy Sterling, whom I'd once saved from getting trampled when she tried to confront a group of drunken centaurs. She, at least, thought I was a hero and not a dangerous beast or meddling freelancer. She greeted me with a smile. "Hey, Vern! The captain's going to be glad to see you."

I snorted.

"No, really." She glanced around to be sure no one was in the foyer, but spoke in a lower voice, anyway. "We brought in this nun. Must be from Faerie 'cause her habit didn't look like any I'd ever seen. Kind of medieval? Anyway, she was fine until they tried to take her personal effects, then she freaked out, started screaming, and the whole place got, I dunno, weird. Like..."

She shrugged, but I understood. To the disappointment of most Mundanes, only Faerie humans could manipulate magic, and then, only those with a charism or the blood of a Magical in their ancestry—or demonic help. Most mortal creatures lacked even the capability to process the sensation of magic; that Tracy felt anything spoke volumes about the power Sister Grace had called to herself. The energy was still there, on standby but slowly dissipating.

"Anyway," she continued, "the captain went in and diffused the situation."

"How? Did he shoot her?" I suspected if he had, I'd have found the entire police station reduced to rubble, but then again, I did not know Sister Grace's level of control.

But Tracy just laughed. "Oh, Vern! He only makes that threat to people with more than two legs. Or hooves. That fawn kind of put him over the edge. No, he stopped Vialpando from tasing her. I heard the yelling even from my desk. I know you guys don't get along, but he really is a good policeman."

I wrinkled my nose in doubt. "I'll believe it when I see it."

"Well, then go see. They're in his office, talking." She buzzed me in.

The main area of the precinct followed the typical "open office" plan, with desks shoved together in twos and fours, detectives on one side, beat cops on the other. Everyone had those privacy films on their screens so that passers-by couldn't read what was on them, but if you needed to interview someone privately, there were room along two walls. I'd been in those a time or twelve. Generally not fun.

Santry didn't get a private office. Instead, he was ensconced in a glassed-in fishbowl of an office in the middle of the right side, with only venetian blinds for privacy. The blinds were down, but half closed in a less-than-effective compromise between privacy and transparency. Sister Grace was in a chair, slouched over a Styrofoam cup that she held with both hands. Santry was in a chair opposite her, leaning toward her and speaking softly.

The sound-absorbing tiles kept the normal chaos of police work to a manageable level, and between it, the still-respectable din of a busy police force, and the closed door of Santry's office, I could not make out what they were saying. But his tone was surprisingly soothing.

I stood there, trying to process this kinder, gentler side of the pain-in-my-tail police chief, a detective noticed me and rapped on the captain's door. Santry glanced up, saw me, and patted Grace's knee. Then he came to me.

"'Bout time you showed up," he grumbled.

Good. I was worried Sister Grace might have put some kind of sweetness glamour on him. 'Course, I'm not sure any mage was that powerful.

"I was in Faerie when I got the message. Then, I had to get bail money—but I'm told I don't need it?"

Santry tsked. "Couple of parents complained to the school. Their precious angel says Sister Grace put a hex on her and she can't sing. Grace says she told the kid to stop singing one particular song."

"Mishmash?"

"God, I hate that song. Had to ban it from the building. So Principal Sandoval decided this was a police matter. Only, there aren't any laws against telling a ten-year-old brat to stop annoying you, and I can't see how telling a child to stop singing is child endangerment—even with magic behind the command." Santry's eyes flashed with anger. He'd been after the city council to pass some laws classifying magic as a weapon.

He continued. "I've called the principal and the family. Told them they'd have to take this up with the school board or sue her if they want to make a point. In the meantime, you take your nun—"

"She's not my nun!"

"She is now. I'm remanding her into your custody. She is a woman on the edge, she's terrified of herself and her own power, and God-only-knows-why, she wants you. So you're going to stick with her until she gets over this or gets out of my town. Or until she does something I can arrest her for."

I gaped a minute at the sheer audacity of the human before me. Who did he think he was, Saint George?

No, but he was a knight and a lord of the land in his own way. Still...

"Am I getting paid?"

Santry snorted. "You're getting paid with your freedom, drake. There may not be laws against the practice of magic yet, but there are against dangerous animals, and I know you've been messing it up with Los Despredatores again. I've got a cage just for you. I've even lined it with straw."

"You're all heart."

Taking that as agreement, his manner calmed. "Look, Vern, I don't know why she thinks you can help, but she needs someone who can understand her, and if that's not you, then find someone for her. That level of PTSD is not something to trifle with, especially since it seems magic is her loaded weapon."

"PTSD?" I asked, and before he could realize this was news to me, I added, "What would you know about PTSD?"

"None of your business," he snapped. "Now will you take responsibility for her, or do I call the hospital and hope things don't get messy?"

Was that pain in his eyes? "Yeah. Yeah, I've got her."

"Good." He spun on his heels and strode to his office. He opened the door and spoke gently to Sister Grace, who set down her tea and straightened her habit. One hand clutching her cross, she slipped the other through his. Together, they exited the building, looking neither right nor left, not even to acknowledge me. With a shrug, I followed.

As I got outside, Sister Grace was thanking him and promising to pray for his father.

He quirked a sad smile. "It's too late for that."

"It's never too late for prayer, Michael."

His smile warmed, and he gave her a small nod. As he passed by me, he muttered, "Take care of her, drake."

And then it was just me, a stressed-out nun, and a munitions-level gathering of magic.

"Shall we go to my place and talk?" I asked. At least if she blew that up, it'd be no big loss.

My "place" was a run-down warehouse in the bad part of town. It was bad even for the area, but it was big, which is probably what Dona Elena was thinking when she left it to me. I missed that feisty mortal. In particular, I missed having the chance to tell her what a dump she'd saddled me with.

I tried to make the best of it. At one point, we tried making a large closet into a bed for me by shutting the bottom half of the door and filling it with all the miniature plush toys we could find. It worked great...until the first rainstorm. Then I discovered not only how much my new lair leaked, but how disgusting it was to wake up immersed in soggy beanie buddies. I will never forget the sound of the squishing. After that, I resigned myself to sleeping on the floor. Thanks to the nightmares, it was now gouged with claw marks and a couple of singes.

So, overall, my lair was not much to look at and completely embarrassing by dragon standards, but it was mine. It actually wasn't half bad when I had friends over, but the days of long afternoons playing Dungeon and Dragons with my gaming friends were gone. I missed the camaraderie.

Maybe that's why when our ride dropped us off and we entered the warehouse, I led her again to the kitchen. I filled the kettle and breathed fire on it until the water boiled. Once I had her settled in with the tea, I asked her to explain what had happened. "Is it true? Did you put a compulsion spell on a child?"

Eyes on the dark swirls in her cup, she nodded.

Dragons can't whistle, so I just scowled. "You've got some temper, sister."

Her face flushed red, and her eyes sparkled. "Is that what you think? That I let a child provoke me? Aye, I'm sure Addison was singing that song because she wanted to annoy me. She can be a most disagreeable child. But that's not why I made her stop."

That song? "Mishmash?"

"Of course, 'Mishmash!' Do ye think I'd have reacted if she sang 'Ode to Joy?' But it wasn't the song, not of itself. Vern, Addison has perfect enunciation and perfect pitch! She kept singing it, perfectly, start to finish, over and over. And the more she sang it, the less she seemed aware of what she was doing. She kept singing it, faster and better and, and I saw..." She closed her eyes, shook her head, banishing the memories. But memories from when?

"What did you see?"

She shivered. "Tentacles."

If dragons could cross their arms over their chests, I'd have done so. "Addison was growing tentacles?"

"No, no. Not like that. They flowed from her mouth, and they covered her from behind. And they reached for me. They were ethereal, like mist. Like dreams..."

She gripped her cross like a lifeline.

"Like flashbacks?" I accused.

She leaned forward, her eyes gone cold and hard. I felt magic gathering around her, like electricity before a lightning strike. She spoke with a tight voice. "I am not imagining this."

"Are you sure?" I tilted my head skeptically. I needed to know what we were dealing with—what I was dealing with—and some instinct said the only way she'd talk to me is if I got her mad enough.

"I hired you to analyze that song, not me!"

Now we were getting somewhere. "Are you sure there's a difference? Why is it no one in Faerie believes you about this song?"

"They don't understand! They aren't here!"

"And no one is coming to investigate, or you would not have involved me in this fiasco. So why don't they trust you? Is it because you're in the Mundane for psychiatric help?"

"That has nothing to do with the song! I'm telling you, there is something evil about that song. We have to find out what it is." The magic rose, reached a crescendo.

I pressed on. "Why me? Why aren't you over there seeking the evidence yourself? Why haven't you gone to Faerie to convince your superiors?"

Show me your temper. I can take it, and I need to know what you are.

"Because I can't return! There's too much magic, too much danger!"

"For whom?"

Then slowly, deliberately, she dissipated the power gathering around her. She set her palms on the cracked Formica of the ancient kitchen table and pushed herself out of her chair. "You were in the Great War. You know what the Enemy can do. I thought you, of all beings..." She took a deep breath, then headed to the door.

I stood and followed. "Where are you going?"

She paused with her hand on the doorknob. "Don't worry. I'll explain it to Captain Santry. I'll continue to pray for you. Keep the money, but you needn't work on this just to humor your client's imagination."

She didn't even slam the door on her way out. Somehow, that only made me feel worse.

Chapter Six: Am I My Sister's Keeper?

I didn't sleep well that night. I kept having the same nightmare. I was at a feast at Bishop Aiden's. A child was on a platter, dressed up like a turkracken, a different child each time, but always with a sneer and a mess of tentacles coming out its orifices. Grace was at one end of the table, praying, her words muffled. She had duct tape on her mouth. The bishop sipped tea and told me I couldn't have any because eating children was a sin. Meanwhile the childracken oozed off the table, octopus-style, and start gnawing on the leg of one of the bishop's pages.

Pretty straightforward as far as nightmares went. Until the emus arrived. I hate emus; like velociraptors minus the teeth. The child would sing that song while the emu army squawked accompaniment and I'd yell for Grace to take off her gag while Bishop Aiden recited the Rules of

Acquisition. Then I'd wake up in the dragon equivalent of a cold sweat, roll over, and start all over again.

I'd just settled into good sleep when my phone rang.

"This better not be about emus," I grumbled to the caller.

"Yeah," Father Rich replied slowly. "And good morning to you, too. Have you seen Sister Grace?"

I glared at my phone. It was only 9:00. "Why are you asking me? Since when did I become my sister's keeper?" I winced. Since Santry made me so yesterday, on pain of incarceration. And I'd let her walk out the door. I sighed and asked grudgingly, "Why are you asking?"

"She didn't show up at school today."

I laughed. "School? You mean where Principal Sandoval had her arrested?"

"Yes," Father said, his voice tinged with exasperation, but whether at me, Grace, the principal, or the whole situation, I could not tell. "Kathy says she panicked and now she wants to apologize."

"Apologize. By having Sister Grace come to the same office where Principal Kathy panicked and had the police haul her away the day before?" I waited for the punch line.

Father didn't supply it. "Sister Grace isn't answering her phone. The police told Kathy that they released her, and you picked her up. I was going to go to her apartment, but I thought I'd check with you first, to make sure she wasn't with you."

I started to protest that this was none of my business, but then I pictured the straw Santry had so graciously bought to line a jail cell. "I'll meet you at her apartment complex."

Being able to take the straight route (by the air) meant I got there before Father did, so I did a quick reconnaissance to look for signs of gathering magic. Everything seemed normal, or as normal as life on the edge of the Gap could be, so I met Father Rich at his car, and together we walked to the front door of the transition home.

"Thanks for coming," Father said as he rang the doorbell. "I just figured, since you and she seem to be getting along..."

"She's a client," I grouched back. "We're not buddies. We haven't bonded. She paid me to do a job, and that money runs out today. She's really none of my business."

Father turned and gave me a querulous look. "Did you do that on purpose?"

It took me a minute to figure out what he meant. None of my business. Nun of my business. I sighed. "Would you believe I'm just tired? Too many nightmares."

"About emus?" Father asked as the door opened to reveal the sharp-suited woman I'd seen while snooping. She looked from me to Father and back to me, and her face broke into a grin.

"Well, there's a conversation to walk in on. Please, welcome." She had a warm accent that said her parents had immigrated from India and that she'd grown up bilingual. She stepped back to let us in, and then shook Father's hand. "Father Rich, it's good to see you again. And you must be Vern, our resident dragon?"

"The one and only."

We forewent the awkwardness of trying to shake hand and claw. She introduced herself as

Dr. Indira Prakash and led us to elevators. Once the doors had closed, she asked, "So why would a dragon have nightmares about emus?"

"They remind me of velociraptors. I hate velociraptors. Vicious creatures. Pack hunters."

"Interesting. Have you been feeling ganged up on lately?"

I snorted. "Every day since I crossed the Gap, Doc."

Father chuckled. "Wow, she got you in one, Vern."

I glared at him, then said, "All right then, Doctor, explain to me why, in my dream, Bishop Aiden was reciting the Rules of Acquisition."

She shrugged. "Sometimes, the brain—well, the human brain—just tosses in recent memories as a way to process information. You haven't been binging Deep Space Nine lately?"

As the elevator doors opened on Father's laughter, I made a note to come to Dr. Prakash whenever I needed help profiling a suspect.

Grace's door looked like any other. Indira knocked on it. "Sister Grace? It's Doctor Prakash. You have visitors."

As I expected, there was no answer, but I let her knock again and Father knock as well before suggesting they call her phone. We heard ringing from inside the apartment.

"I have a master key," Indira said, her voice tinged with worry.

Grace's apartment was spartan but...

Nah. Spartan pretty much covered it. And not even in the vow-of-poverty way like you'd expect in a cloister. Aside from a couple of pictures on the bulletin board, obviously drawn by the schoolchildren who liked her, there was little else to indicate anyone lived there. The bed was neatly made. A single habit hung in the closet, a pair of winter boots waited tucked in the corner. Several bottles stood like sentinels on the dresser.

While Indira checked Grace's phone to see who she contacted last, I sauntered to the dresser, picked up a bottle, noted the refill date and directions, and counted the pills. Wherever she was going, she took a five-day supply with her. I peeked in the drawers and the side table. Her breviary was there, as were school papers she was working on. I debated opening the diary and decided that went beyond what I was paid for.

In the living room, a harp leaned against the wall, still in its case. I didn't see dust on it, but I suspected it had not been touched since it was set there. I didn't see any sheet music, either.

By the time Indira announced that Grace hadn't called anyone since the taxi that took her home last night, I already had a fair idea of where she'd gone and why. The question now was: How much do I share?

"She left her phone, so she probably isn't planning on being gone long," Indira was saying to Father. "Maybe she simply went on a long walk. We encourage our residents to take awareness walks when they're feeling overwhelmed."

"What would she be overwhelmed about?" I asked casually as I poked my nose into drawers and pretended to sniff under the bed. It was as clean as the rest of the room.

There was a long pause before Indira said, "I can't really discuss it. Patient-doctor confidentiality."

I grunted. PIs and priests also had something similar, which was going to get in the way of us helping each other. But could she help?

"Did she call you, 'Indira'?" I asked.

Again that hesitation, then her face fell. "No. No, she was always very formal."

I shrugged. "Don't take it personally. So where do your residents like to take these 'awareness walks'? I'll go search around. I'll bet I can find her."

Thus reassured, Indira escorted us out. Father, however, knew me better. We walked in silence to his car, but before he got in, he said, "You don't think she went on a walk."

"Actually, I do," I replied, "but not on some aimless wander to work off stress. She packed for a few days. If I don't contact you this evening, you might want to let Indira and the school know that she'll be gone for a while."

"What's she doing?"

"Taking my advice," I said but refused to answer further. After another assurance that I'd find her and make sure she was okay, Father got into his car and left. Then, I launched myself into the air and took off for the Gap. Somewhere in Faerie was a stressed-out nun with a music obsession and a dire need to prove herself. And if my suspicions were right, she was a magical mine just needing the right jostling to go off.

St. Scholastica Catholic School was along my route to the Gap. A large crowd of adults was gathered on the front stoop, along with camera crews. There were hostile chants about magic having no part in their school. Grace's name was mentioned. To the side, a news team was interviewing two angry parents, who stood with their hands on the shoulders of a sniffling girl. Addison.

I gained altitude and hurried past before someone caught sight of me. Given the mood of the crowd, no one was going to care that I was a guest at Addison's class's Show and Tell just last week.

I sighed. This was just great. People were finally starting to get used to magic—used to me. Now, all that progress was going to be destroyed by one little snot-nosed child who was playing the adults for attention. If she was exaggerating. Santry thought so, but he wouldn't know magic if it bit him on the nose. Besides, I would not have put it past him to let this go as a way to force the council to make some laws concerning the use of magic. He liked clear guidelines.

Grace said Addison was exaggerating the breadth of the spell, that she'd only told her to stop singing a song that was hurting her, but what evidence did I have that she was right and not just imagining things?

I had to get to the bottom of this before the whole situation exploded. Which meant I had to figure out Sister Grace.

Santry had said she had PTSD. That presumes some kind of traumatic experience in her past, but what? She didn't look older than 32, but that didn't mean anything. The fact that she could manipulate magic at all meant she had to have some Magical ancestry. The old fairy tales about magical creatures taking human form to mate with humans was true. So Grace could be the child of a long-lived species and as a result looked far younger than she was. I didn't sense anything elvish about her; not that I could see her ears under her wimple, but usually elvish stock ran tall and willowy. Still, there were plenty of long-lived Magical species. Had she only recently discovered her power, perhaps by reflexively casting some destructive spell?

I shook my head as I angled toward the Gap. No, that didn't feel right. She would not have been so calm and sure about what had happened with Addison. And Santry said she'd freaked out when they tried to put her in a holding cell, not at the scene.

And what about Santry? She didn't call her psychologist by first name (and everyone did; I knew from hours of eavesdropping), yet she called the guy who was responsible for her arrest "Michael" and promised to pray for him. Plus, he knew her condition, something she obviously kept private. Had she told him, or had he guessed? Either way, she seemed more comfortable with him than the counselor who'd spent six months trying to help her.

I paused my mental deliberations as I came upon the Gap port. The Gap itself was a large portal roughly circular in shape. There were no definite edges, but a kind of fraying barrier as the hole in the space-time continuum reached its limit and the Mundane dimension imposed its dominion. The Gap itself was not much to look at. Unlike the watery-flushing image of the Stargate or the brilliant swirling colors of other science fiction, it looked, according to a popular American magazine, "nothing so much as a burlap curtain some deep-woods redneck might hang in their window to keep out flies. But in this case, the 'curtain' is 40 feet in diameter and does nothing to protect us from the pests on the other side."

Yeah. "Pests." Insulting metaphors aside, the writer was accurate about one thing: The gap did look dull and plain to human eyes. It was really too bad they couldn't see it like dragons do. I could gaze at the complex designs of interacting energies for hours...if someone didn't try to shoo me away. Like a pest. Go figure.

The author was also right in that the Gap did not discriminate. While magic only came through in a trickle, anything corporeal had free access: good, evil, wild, tame. Well, almost anything. The nature of Gap spells had screens to keep some things from seeping through, like mosquitos and airborne diseases. Otherwise, Faerie would have been dealing with a lot more trouble with plagues than it does. However, anything that could make a conscious decision to travel through the "burlap curtain" didn't have any problem.

Which meant the governments on both sides stepped in to police what entered their respective universes. On the Faerie side there's an interlocking set of spells and repulsions set up. Those with harmful intent have to work hard to cross into the Mundane. (Many managed it, of course, or I'd be out of a job.)

Of course, on the Mundane side, we got the Gap Security Authority.

The Gap Port was a large, wide structure mostly dedicated to long lines and shops to help you spend your money before entering long lines. People were scanned and asked questions by bored staff members before moving along to a wide hallway that led to the Gap. To the south were roads where trucks or carts of trade goods could be inspected before moving on. The nature of the Gap prevented it from being closed in— although the Mundanes did try—but the area was fenced in, patrolled, and designated a No-Fly/No-Drone zone.

Of course, being me, I ignored that last. At first, the port authorities shot at me. Now, they've resigned themselves to token protests and shaking fists.

But not today. I had to find Grace.

First, I did a circuit of the area, checking for her scent and any disruptions of magic that might indicate her presence.

I passed by a huge construction site, now abandoned for the winter. I wondered briefly if Grace might hide there. The area was as large as a subdivision, but whatever they were building was too crowded together to be houses. Plenty of spots to lay low.

No. She'd gone somewhere with purpose. That meant Faerie.

I landed outside the door of the Gap terminal where a large sign declared, "Be Kind to Our Faerie Neighbors! No iron beyond this point." Below was a list of prohibited metal objects, some of which weren't necessary, and some of which were added on after experience taught us they were. To the side was a shop where you could rent or purchase plastic walkers and wheelchairs.

The duke hadn't liked a state senator who had a limp, and thus decided to prohibit metal canes from crossing into Faerie. Then, in a show of kindness, he presented said senator with a hand carved walking stick that was two inches too short and covered with "Ancient runes" which was really a secret code he and his brother had made up as kids and which described a dirty limerick.

Well, somehow his joke became understood as a prohibition on all ambulatory assistance devices that contained metal. But of course, capitalism won in the end.

I paused at the metal detector and gave the attendant a toothy grin. He barely blinked.

"If you have any metal artifacts or prohibited items, you must leave them here," the attendant said in a bored voice. "There are lockers provided for a small fee in Guest Services. Please step forward slowly through the device. Move at a deliberate pace, neck and tail extended horizontally, two feet on the pad at a time only."

"Did you work yesterday?" I asked.

"Once your entire length has cleared the scanner... I, uh. Yeah, I did. Why?"

"Did a nun come through during your shift? Deep blue habit? Distinctive triangular sleeves?"

"Trumpet sleeves, you mean? Yeah, she came through, about four, maybe? I had to use the wand to check the sleeves."

"She seem upset?"

He shrugged. "Not especially, but then again, lots of people get upset at me. I'm really good at tuning them out."

"You're a credit to your profession."

"Whatever. There's a line behind you. Please step forward."

"Nah. I'll take the short cut." Sister Grace had a 16-hour head start on me. I was going to need a miracle to find her as it was.

I launched myself into the air and was through the Gap before the guards had a chance to shake their fists.

Chapter Seven: Nunwhere to Run To

The weather on the Mundane side of the Gap was sunny, clear, and 72 degrees. Naturally, the Faerie side was in the middle of a frigid thunderstorm. A violent gust of wind smacked me sideways as I exited the Gap, sending me into a spin. For once, my small size was to my advantage, as I was able to tuck, roll, then furl my wings and ascend without smacking the ground. The wind wasn't letting me off that easy, though. It shoved me farther and farther from the Gap guards I'd planned on questioning, all the while pelting me with stinging rain that blurred my vision and messed with my sense of smell.

After lightning raced directly across my path and a third blast of wind knocked me for a loop, I gave in to the inevitable. It wasn't like I'd find Grace in this torrent, anyway. If she were anywhere nearby, she was probably holed up some-where with a warm fire and tea.

A warm fire didn't sound like a bad idea, but there weren't any caves nearby. There was, how-ever, a small chapel run by the Silent Brothers. I'd spent a hundred years with their order before crossing the Gap. They might have something to warm me up. If nothing else, I could get out of the rain. I banked and angled eastward, manag-ing to land with some grace despite the gusts and low visibility.

I pushed the heavy doors open and slipped through as quickly as I could. The doors shut with a low, soft thud, and the sound of the rains muted to a dull roar. I stood dripping and fighting the urge to shake myself as I took in my surroundings.

The chapel had been built specifically for the Gap, as a place for visitors, residents, and those who worked around the Gap to come and wor-ship. Two lines of pews a dozen deep led to the sanctuary, where a large, wooden crucifix hung behind the altar. I had known the artist back in the day; chances were, I'd even hauled that par-ticular log back for him to work his skills upon.

There were a few people, kneeling in prayer or sitting as they waited for the storm to pass. Their voices were muted, and their forms shadowy in the dim light of the chapel.

Then lightning flashed, and the entire chapel flared with multicolored light from the stained glass. Almost immediately, thunder followed, booming like the Wrath of God. Everyone jumped.

Everyone except for a nun in a blue habit with trumpet sleeves kneeling before the statue of Our Lady of Miracles reaching out to St. Sabrina, the founder of the order.

I glanced to the right to the statue of St. Borthal, Patron Saint of the Miraculous Happenstance. I gave him an appreciative nod.

Just then a side door opened, and a priest in homespun robes approached me, towels in hand. A Silent Brother, though not someone I knew. He nodded, then gently dried my head and crouched down. I let him wipe my feet. After he'd set the soggy cloths to the side, I asked him about the sister who was in such fervent prayer.

She had been there since yesterday, he told me in the simple, cryptic signing of his order.

She'd come in upset and not moved from that spot. She'd refused food but did accept some water to take some pills.

I nodded my thanks, then went to join her, the clacking of my nails a sharp staccato against the steady low roar of the rain and occasional rumble of thunder. In the pews, a couple of folks glanced my way, and I saw one woman clandestinely reach for her phone. Grace, however, kept her eyes pinned on the smiling, carved face of the sainted founder of her order. I could sense the magic around her, but here in Faerie, it didn't feel as sharp as it did in the Mundane.

I settled myself next to her. She ignored me. I flexed my shoulders, rearranged my wings… Pawed the floor. Nothing. You'd have thought she was made of the same stone as the statue.

I leaned toward her. "So," I drawled, "is this storm your doing?"

Her eyes darted to glare sideways at me. "What?"

I shrugged innocently. "Just checking."

Then I settled in to join my prayers to hers as we waited out the storm.

I cycled through all the mysteries of the rosary, including the miraculous ones, which the Mundane Vatican hadn't recognized, but which were a part of the Faerie Church. I was meditating on the multiplication of the loaves and fishes as the rain started to ease up. By the time I got to the raising of Lazarus from the dead, it had stopped altogether. Around us, visitors wrapped up their own meditations, thanked their wordless host, and left. A few put some money in the poor box as they went.

"Well," I asked Grace when the last one had left and the priest had tidied up and gone to the back, "where to next?"

"Next?" She blinked at me in confusion, and I didn't think it was because I was including myself in her plans.

"Unless you intended to hide away from the worlds. I did that for a hundred years, you know. It gets old, fast. Besides, there's trouble brewing in the Mundane, and some of that is your fault. I can't fix it alone."

Her eyes shimmered with tears in the candlelight. She turned back to the icon of her order's founder. "I just want it all to end." She whispered her plea.

How cryptic and unhelpful. I turned to face her directly, and when she refused to look at me, I set my tail on her shoulder and forced her to face me.

"Listen, Sister," I said with as much kindness as my mounting impatience allowed. "You could have gone to your order, but you came to me. When you got arrested, you could have called your psych, but you called me. Everybody, including you, wants me to make you my business. So here I am, but if you want my help, you have to help me."

She frowned. "I told you. I don't expect anything more. Keep the money."

I snorted. "Your money ran out yesterday. I'm here for...enlightened self-interest. I don't like pre-adolescent brats wreaking havoc in my town, I don't want to end up in Santry's jail cell, and I'm still not convinced that there's nothing to this song obsession of yours."

Now, I really had her confused. "You're not? Yesterday, you said..."

"I didn't 'say' anything. I asked a lot of questions—in an insulting tone, granted, but you don't open up easily, do you? And I wanted to know if you'd actually lash out in anger. But you didn't. And if you wouldn't compel a dragon to shut up because he was questioning your sanity, I doubt you'd hex a child to stop singing just because she's annoying. So, you saw something that scared you into action. I believe that. The question is, did it come from the song or your imagination? I think you're always scared. You hide it under a kind of formal politeness to others, and anger around me..."

"I'm sorry."

I shrugged. "I can handle it. And you know that, or you'd approach me with the same gentle aloofness you do everyone else. Except Santry. That was weird."

"Michael's a good man. I think you and he are more alike than you care to admit."

I blanched. Me and that overzealous Knight in a Bad Suit? I decided to deflect the issue. "Are you saying you have a type?"

She snickered, the first genuinely relaxed thing I'd seen her do since we'd met. "I suppose. I do feel I can trust him."

"So can I, to be a pain in my tail at every possible opportunity," I said, making her giggle again. It was a nice, melodious giggle, with a hint of something Magical I could not trace. I filed that away for later. "Never mind. So you trust him. How much do you trust me? I get the feeling you told him more in the hour you were in his office than you've told me in the week we've known each other."

"You're right. I'm sorry."

"I don't need apologies. I need answers. We need answers."

She glanced again to the statue, then to me, then to the floor. I refrained from tapping my claws in annoyance. I think she realized that I would no longer accept half-efforts. Once she accepted, she was all-in.

For that matter, so was I. What was I getting into? I had not forgotten the genie's prophecy of a year ago. He'd said I'd find grace and no longer be alone. I'd told him he sounded like a Christian fortune cookie, yet here was Grace, in the most literal form possible. And, despite our fights, I had the feeling that we could be friends. But at what price?

I'd rather be alone than spend the next few decades being the angst-sponge of a depressed religious.

Finally, she glanced around the chapel. "Can we find somewhere to talk?"

As if summoned, the priest shuffled to us, and with hand gestures and welcoming smiles, bade us to retire to another room. That was the thing about the Silent Brothers: closed mouths, open ears. Grace leaned heavily on the kneeler as she rose. Her face grimaced with discomfort as she forced her legs to straighten.

"How long were you praying?" I asked.

She shrugged and accepted the priest's assistance with a smile of thanks. "I don't know. Since I crossed the Gap."

"That was over 15 hours." I let her use me for support as we walked toward the narthex.

"I lost track of time. The Lord is my comfort."

"I think the psalmist said he made you to lie down in green pastures, though."

She stopped leaning on me long enough to smack my flank, but I saw the grin she tried to suppress.

Her legs loosened up quickly, and by the time we got to the small kitchen, she was walking smoothly. We accepted tea and bread from the priest, then he bowed to us and left.

"So you spent time with the Silent Brothers?" Grace said conversationally as she poured us each tea. She held my bowl of tea questioningly, and I indicated with a nod that I was fine with it at the table. Then she broke us some bread, and with a nod of permission from me, buttered my piece and set it before me. "Did you spend much time lying in verdant pastures?"

"I spent most of my time plowing the verdant pastures."

"Penance for eating their ox?"

It wasn't just a tease. She was warming up to something. Well, if I expected her to open up, maybe I needed to do some sharing first. "It was after the Great War. I was recovering. I'd...ingested a cursed artifact. It was the only way I had to destroy it. I didn't have my fire then. Didn't have a lot of things."

"And ill from the artifact, with all that evil literally leeching into your system. It could not have been easy. How did you deal with it?"

"A lot of plow pulling. A lot of feeling sorry for myself. Time."

"Did it frighten you? The evil inside you?"

I shook my head. "Mostly, I was too busy feeling sorry for myself. All that energy I needed to heal took me back centuries in my progress toward becoming my whole self."

Sister Grace tore a chunk off her bread, but even though it'd been nearly a day since she'd eaten, she did not bring the morsel to her mouth. "I'm afraid. Afraid all the time. Afraid that there's evil inside me that I can't see and won't be able to control."

"Were you cursed?" I asked, but she continued, either not hearing or not ready to answer.

"They'll use my voice. Demons are so good at twisting gifts. That's why I won't sing, not any longer. It's too risky. My order thought if I went to the Mundane, away from magic…"

She paused to grin, a sad, wistful smile of dead wishes and broken dreams. "It did for a bit. My fears eased. I found my voice. I even sang in the choir at the National Cathedral. I enjoyed the east coast. I thought I might go farther north, Maine, perhaps, start again in a quiet parish by the sea."

"But you couldn't. You had to return to the Gap or die."

She nodded. It was a hard-learned fact that anyone with Magical blood needed a steady infusion of Faerie magic to stay alive. It was like a nutrient we took from the air, or maybe photosynthesis was a closer analogy. Either way, get a Magical too far from the Gap for too long and we get seriously ill.

I wondered how much Magical blood Grace had in her lineage, and where it came from, but this was not the time to ask. She was talking about how coming back, being around magic, had stirred up her old fears, and she couldn't take the chance of losing control of her ability.

"But you did," I pointed out. "You sing-songed a geas on a little girl to make her stop singing a particular song."

"I had to!" Her eyes flared, as did the magic around us, yet not in the same way it had in Los Lagos. There, it had gathered, pressing, begging to be used. Here, it simply reacted to her outburst, the way a surge of current might make a lightbulb burn brighter.

I held up a claw. "That's my point. You made a conscious decision and enacted a very limited, controlled spell in an effort to protect a child from what you perceived as a threat. And, fears aside, you don't seem to regret it."

She stared into her tea as she considered my words. "No," she mused. "I don't suppose that I do. But I do regret having to do it. Which comes back to the song. We have to stop it. It's growing stronger. I can feel it."

"What, the song?"

"Yes! Somewhat? It's more everything around the song. I know others are singing it—and singing it perfectly. There's a rising tension."

"Sure it's not you?"

She flopped back in her chair and crossed her arms. She gave me an equally cross look. "We're back to that again, are we?"

"We never left. I get that you're afraid of using your magic, and I gather that you shape spells with your voice. You were or think you were cursed. What's that got to do with Santry saying you have PTSD or the anti-anxiety medication hidden in your sleeves? What's it got to do with tentacles?"

"Tentacles?"

"You know, like you saw coming out of Addison's mouth and that were threatening to swallow her up? Were you attacked by a sea monster as a child? Or did you almost drown, get tangled in seaweed, or...?"

Then, she did something I did not expect. She burst out laughing.

Chapter Eight: Nunwhere to Hide

"Would it surprise you, Vern, to learn that I was a willful child?" Grace asked.

"Not particularly."

She smirked in reply and fingered the table-cloth, tugging the threads around a hole in the lace. "I took after my papa that way. He and my mother were artisans; he of metal, she of lace, the best in the county. When I was a wee lass, he moved us to Dublin, where we'd find a better market for their wares. My grandmother begged him not to go. 'Twas a geas on my family, you see, that no child set foot in the sea until after their First Communion. The brideprice my great-grandmother paid to become human and marry my great-grandfather."

"She was a siren?" That explained a little, but not much. "I take it you went swimming?"

"My father had been away on a trip. I think he was fetching my grandparents. I don't remember. I was four at the time, I think, and I was always his princess. I missed him terribly. So when I saw his ship, I slipped away from my nanny, dove into the sea, and begged him to come play with me. In the water. They pulled me onto the boat, and I was so angry. I wanted back in the water. So I sang. I was only four, but I started a riot. People were hurt."

She paused then, and I watched as her fingers played with the strings, weaving them through the other loops to fill the gap in the pattern. It was clumsy work, even given that she didn't have a needle. I hadn't seen any lacework in her apartment. Had she been sent away, then? Had she understood why?

Dragons didn't have parents, but I did know what it was like to be torn from family. "It wasn't your fault," I ventured.

"Wasn't it?" she mused. "I was too young to understand, mayhaps, but I disobeyed my parents and my nanny. My own grandmother knocked me out cold. But that's not the point.

I've nothing to fear from the sea or the creatures in it.

"The sisters took me in, hobbled my powers and my voice until they could train me. They gave me a family that not even my blood family could match. I am content with how I came to be in the Order of Our Lady of Miracles."

"And yet, you don't sing," I said.

She flinched, pulling a run in the lace. "That...came later."

"And does *that* have to do with tentacles?"

She smacked her hand on the table. Her cup bounced, sloshing the tea inside. "For the last time, Vurnerrah! I did not imagine them. I am not delusional. I'm not looking at Addison and seeing my younger self. She's a Mundane—and I was willful, selfish, even, but never mean-spirited. When she sang, her only motivation was to get on my nerves.

"That song is calling something. Something deep. Something evil. And we have got to stop it."

"All right." I shrugged. "Let's go see your order. Finish your tea."

I got up and started for the door, giving her just enough time to swallow down the cold liquid. I let her leave first, but as she passed under the threshold, I said, "Maybe you should fix that?"

With my tail, I pointed to the knotty, lopsided hem of the tablecloth.

She sighed ruefully at her handiwork. "Even as a child my mother despaired of my fingerwork." She fixed the lace with a cantrip.

A cantrip she sang.

Interesting.

Sister Grace thanked the priest, and I did the same. We never asked his name, but that was okay. It was the way of the Silent Brothers; they took remaining "unspotted by the world" very seriously. On the way out, I shoved a couple of twenties into the poor box. I had been planning to use it in my search for Sister Grace, anyway.

The sky was clear and blue and just a little chillier than a Medsea drake like me found comfortable, but everything sparkled with clinging raindrops and looked clean and new. Except the road from the chapel back to civilization. I grimaced with distaste as my feet squished in the cold mud. Fortunately, the Faerie were not as particular about lawns as Mundanes. I wiped my feet in the grass while Sister Grace laughed. I noticed she had no problems walking in the muddy road. The filth slid off her shoes and habit.

"You want to teach me that trick?" I asked as I walked beside her, sticking to the grass. A narrow bed of pansies lined the road, their sweet smell rising between us. Already, the sun was starting to warm the air, evaporating the last of the moisture.

Grace ambled along, wearing a small smile as she tilted her face to the sun. If she had been terrified of returning to Faerie, that fear had vanished with the storm. Or was it because of me?

More likely, it was 15 hours of prayer and a strong cup of tea. I'd chide myself for being so arrogant, but I was a dragon, after all.

Regardless, she seemed more comfortable than I'd ever seen her. The birds had begun to sing, and I had the ridiculous vision of Sister Grace frolicking among them like a fairy tale princess, her voice trilling along with theirs. I wondered if she could out-sing them, and if so, would some ambitious bluebird explode trying to match her range?

I shook my head. Probably not the best scene to bring up.

"What?" Grace asked.

"Glad to see you're feeling better," I said.

"I do," she admitted. "I feel...safer."

"Not like there's some evil in you clawing to get out?"

A shadow of grief clouded her eyes; then it was gone. She turned her gaze back to the road, the grass, the trees. "Not for the moment," she answered airily.

We had half a mile before we got to the Gap port, where we could pick up transportation to her order. And she seemed in a more talkative mood. So, as long as we were sharing... "Why would you think there is evil inside you, anyway? You're a religious; surely, you go to Confession regularly. You say you don't harbor any hidden resentment from your childhood. You do understand that sirens aren't evil, just... instinctual."

"Sirens, like humans, are a Fallen species," she replied. "Their instincts can be turned to evil, and their talents twisted."

"You were a child," I protested again, "who missed her father."

But she shook her head. "This was many, many years later," she said, then changed the subject to the weather and the storms she'd known growing up in Faerie Ireland.

I took the hint and shared a few tales of wild storms I'd flown in. I was just finishing a funny—well, funny, now—story about a storm Zeus had set to dog me for two solid weeks as revenge for a trick my twin and I had played on him...

I stopped, bemused for other reasons.

"What is it?"

"That was before George. But I remember it."

"Do ye think it has to do with the song?" she asked, a hint of nervousness in her voice.

I thought for a minute, then shook my head.

She shrugged, and I could sense her relief. "Count your blessings then."

When we got to the edge of town. We flagged down a wagon that was only too glad to take us to the next town. No griping about upholstery or admonishments about not sticking my head out the window, here.

"I know so little about dragons. They were before my time," Grace said as we left the traffic of the tourist area and the cart picked up its pace. The clopping of the horse's hooves on the hardened dirt of the road made a steady beat to go with the rattle-and-squeak of the wagon wheels. Grace paused and closed her eyes to listen. "It's a music all its own," she said.

I didn't find it especially melodious, but I had to admit, I did enjoy the relative quiet. Los Lagos always seemed full of the whooshing of cars, the squeal of brakes, the background hum of the computer, even the electricity running from the electric pole to my beggarly lair had a tone I had learn to tune out. Fortunately, dragons had talented ears. I wondered aloud how sensitive Grace's ears were.

"They're human enough," she replied when I asked. "Although my great-grandfather was deaf. The cold sea had taken his hearing at a young age. Which, of course, is what saved his life when he met my great-grandmother. The Mundane is noisy, though. And so mechanical. D.C. is so much worse than Los Lagos. But I'd forgotten the sounds of Faerie."

"Forgotten? How long has it been?"

"Five years in November," she said.

If dragons could whistle, I would have. That was just a few years after the opening of the Gap, and not long after things had been "settled" politically between Faerie and Mundane governments and the Catholic churches. It was also longer than I found in her records. Where had she been in those missing years?

Before I could ask, she added, "But yesterday was the first time I'd been on my own in Faerie in a very, very long time. Thank you for coming to find me."

So I *was* the reason for her improved mood. I had to stop selling myself short. "Why are you afraid to be here alone?"

For a long time, she didn't answer. We rode in silence as she looked out the window, played with the hem of her trumpet sleeves. She pulled out her rosary and fingered the beads, but I didn't think she was praying.

I waited, daydreaming ridiculous reasons for why a border guard would know the term trumpet sleeves while I gave her time to gather her nerve. The horses trotted on, their clop-clop-clop a soothing sound, but Grace was no longer relaxed. When I'd exhausted my scenarios and she still hadn't answered, I pressed, "Well?"

"It's...a long story."

"It's a long ride."

She nodded. Her watch, the one piece of technology she wore and incongruous with her medievalish garb, buzzed. She glanced at it, reached into her sleeve for one of her pills, and swallowed it dry.

"We can play Twenty Questions if it will help," I said. "I'll start. What's with those pills?"

Instead, she answered with a question of her own. "Why is it so important to you?"

I gave her a smile that was full of teeth. "I'm a curious wyrm. I don't know who I'm working with or what any of this has to do with that song, and my instincts are telling me I need to know. Besides, I think you want to tell me. You need to tell someone because those pills aren't enough."

Her expression twisted into something between surprise and anger. Then she crossed her arms, flopped her head against the back of the seat, and shut her eyes. I thought she was going to retreat into sleep, when she again answered with a question. "How old do you think I am?"

Sister Grace had a sweet face with pale unblemished skin and a light spattering of freckles that spoke of red hair beneath her wimple. The lines at the corner of her eyes and mouth and on her forehead spoke more of years of pain than years of time. A Mundane would have guessed her in her 30s, but with siren blood, that estimate could be off by a century or more.

I didn't answer, and again, silence stretched until she broke it. "You're not the only one who suffered in the Great War, Vurnerrah. Unfortunately for me, quiet sulking and time could not help."

Ouch. I let the barb slide. "Tell me."

She pressed her lips together, and all her pain lines deepened. Beneath closed lids, her eyes moved. I didn't know whether she was seeking comfort in her mind or lost in a bad memory.

Her rosary lay discarded on the seat beside her. I picked it up with my tail and pressed it against her hand. When she grasped it, I twined my tail around her grip.

"You are not alone."

She released some of her tension with a shuddering sigh. "But I was. They wanted my voice. My power. They tried everything to twist it to their commands. I fought. I prayed. Eventually, I was rescued. But I don't know. I can't know if they succeeded. If they...planted something in me. How can I know? I was alone. I was so alone."

She shivered, and a tear escaped her closed lids.

I didn't have enough answers, but the time for questions was done. I slid off my seat and sat on the floor with my head resting, doglike, in her lap. After a while, she laid her free hand on my head. I let her rub the scales between my horns until we both dozed off.

Chapter Nine: Nun the Wiser

The Stanshire-on-Tweed convent of the Order of Our Lady of Miracles was dedicated to magical research, which meant it was well away from the nearest town with great fields and woods separating it from non-magical civilization. Magical creatures lived in the woods, drawn there by the abundance of ambient magic in the area. Centaurs patrolled the area, watching for any twists of magic, dangerous wildlife, and poachers.

The convent itself sat on a low rise, surrounded by a high wall you could see from the road and a magical barrier I could sense from a mile away. Sister Grace seemed to sense it, too, for she started to tense up as we turned to the narrow road leading to the gate. Our driver didn't seem to have any cares; he whistled a merry tune as the horses ambled along.

At the gate, I paid him the last of my money in Faerie coin. He doffed his hat respectfully, accepted Sister Grace's blessing, and with a sharp whistle set his team back down the road. After a moment, we heard him break into song, the tune and words of which sounded suspiciously like a Faerie remix of "Stairway to Heaven."

I shrugged. At least it wasn't "Mishmash."

Grace stared at the tall wooden gate—or, more accurately, at the magical shielding covering the gate. Her hands were hidden in her sleeves, but I didn't need to see them to know she was trembling.

"This is a research facility," she said, and I couldn't tell if she was reassuring herself or giving voice to her fears.

It didn't matter. We were here, and we were going in.

I said, "Perfect for our mission, then," and pulled the cord to ring the bell.

I heard the faint rustle of someone rising and brushing dirt off her habit, then footsteps. A moment later, the small door in the gate opened and a young human nun with silver-flecked eyes peeked out. She barely noted Sister Grace before turning all her attention on me. Her already large eyes widened, and her mouth puckered into a small 'o.'

Then she slammed the door. We heard her scampering away, calling, "Mother Superior! Mother Superior!"

Grace blinked at me.

I shrugged modestly. "I have that effect sometimes."

"To make people run away screaming? Aye, I suppose that makes sense."

It sounded like something Father Rich would have said—or any of my other Mundane friends. If it had been anyone else, I would have snarked back. But somehow, Sister Grace said it with such honesty, as if it truly had not occurred to her before. And that struck me as incredibly funny. I burst out laughing, and soon, she joined me.

We were still giggling when the gates opened, and we were invited in. Sister Grace passed through the shields without any hesitation.

We were escorted—by my screaming nun, no less, though she seemed more awestruck than terrified—directly to a small side chapel where Mother Superior was sitting, a book on her lap but her silver eyes focused on the entrance, awaiting us. We'd apparently interrupted her quiet time. Nonetheless, she received us graciously. I took a seat in the aisle, and Grace sat beside her in the front pew. Our escort made her exit slowly, walking backward most of the time. Her eyes stayed locked on me, and I could see words straining to leave her lips. But instead, she got to the end of the aisle, genuflected quickly, then dashed out the door without so much as a delighted "eep."

We introduced ourselves, and Sister Grace pulled out a rolled-up copy of the song and explained her suspicions.

"Let no one sing it," Grace warned, "especially those with a perfect pitch."

Mother Superior frowned. "It reads like no summoning I've ever seen. How can you be sure?"

Every muscle in Grace's body tensed with her need to be believed, and it came out in the strain of her voice. "I just am, and I cannot tell ye why. Please, it's becoming very popular in the Mundane, and there's nothing we can do to stop it. We have to be ready for..." She stopped to shrug helplessly. I could almost feel her biting back the assertion that she was not crazy.

But Mother Superior had either never heard about Grace's past or had seen something in the song. She rolled up the papers and set them aside. "We've worked with dangerous artifacts before. We'll be careful."

She turned her silver-eyed gaze upon Grace— or rather around and over Grace's body. "But now, what about you? You wear the habit of our order, but magic twists and frays around you so. You have been wounded, and terribly. How can we help you?"

Grace's lips trembled, but they formed into a warm, grateful smile. "It's alright, Mother. I hie from McCullough convent. They've done all they can."

"They would be the experts. Yet, it's not been enough."

Grace cleared her throat. "No. I'm nae sure anything will be."

Mother Superior reached out as if to cup Grace's cheek in her hand, but she stopped centimeters from her skin, as if comforting the magic that strained toward Grace and was repelled. "With God, there is hope. And God works in His own time, not ours. You shall be our guests tonight. We will speak more of this and pray together."

Grace nodded.

Mother Superior turned to me. "Friend Dragon, we've only a few sheep for wool and a couple of milking cows, but the woods are good for hunting—unless you prefer to rest by the hearth and sup with us later?"

It had been a long time since I was so politely told to go away. I bowed my head regally. "A hunt in the woods sounds like a wonderful change of pace, thank you."

"Sister Eloise can escort you to the back gate. We shall see you at Compline."

Sister Eloise turned out to be our wide-eyed guide from earlier. When I emerged alone from the chapel, she stared at me like St. Peter had come down and handed her the keys to the Pearly Gates.

"Sister Eloise?" I asked, anyway, just to see if she'd explode from happiness. Instead, she smashed her lips together and nodded with quick jerks.

"I'm going to catch my supper. Would you show me the way out?"

Again, the quick nods, followed by a very awkward couple of moments where she curtsied, then started forward, then hesitated, unsure whether she should lead or follow. She looked at me, then raised her foot as if to step again, but paused, watching me intently. Her face got pinker and pinker.

It had to be a sin to have so much fun at Sister Discomfiture's expense, so I swung my nose to indicate that she precede me. She skipped a little before resuming a more sedentary, nun-like pace. We made our way down the hallway, the only sounds the echoes of her footsteps and the clicking of my claws against the stone floors. She cast sidelong glances at me and bit her lip the whole time. By the time we got to the exit, she was practically vibrating.

I decided to give her a break. "You're welcome to speak with me," I said in a compassionate but regal manner. Who was I to break her illusions?

"You're Vurnerrah!" The declaration burst forth like waters breaking from a dam, and the deluge followed. "Vurnerrah, the Great Dragon,

Defender of Mortalkind, who left his own people to join the Church in the battle against evil. My grandmother told us the tales!"

"Oh?" I said, but she was already regurgitating the stories as told by, apparently, my second biggest fan. Grandma had kept up on my adventures before, during, and after the Great War, and then embellished them. Apparently, I alone saved entire towns, defeated full armies of demons, rescued the pope himself on more than one occasion... Seriously, if I weren't a dragon, I would have been embarrassed.

Not that some of it wasn't true, of course. Even diminished, I am a force to be reckoned with, but usually, I was one soldier in God's armies. I tried to tell Sister Fangirl, but she just sighed about my humility and was off again on another wild tale her grandmother had told her.

I let her. It was a refreshing change from the usual blasé attitude Mundanes had for me...when they weren't wondering if I was housebroken and tame. (Housebroken, yes; tame? Ask again if I'm housebroken and find out.) Besides, Sister Recitations wasn't giving me a chance to get a word in edgewise. I began to wonder if she was part

High Elf. They are as longwinded as they are long-lived.

By the time we got to the gate, she was panting—not from the walk, mind you, but from the monologue. She caught her breath as she pulled out the gate keys from the long chain in her pocket. I saw the sparkle of magic on them. As she held the correct key between her fingers, she grew quiet.

"This is the gate. The grounds are just beyond. There are lots of rabbits, and the elk have been plentiful this year."

"Excellent. I'll be back for Compline," I promised. "Will you meet me here?"

"Oh, it would be an honor, but it's my day to prepare the chapel. Besides, it's not really necessary. If I may?"

She settled the key on the crown of my head, between my horns, and whispered a spell. I felt the tingle of magics travel along my scales. It tickled in a way only a dragon would understand, so I refrained from laughing.

Once it was done, she pulled away, smiling. "Now the gates will recognize you as a friend and let you in. Just touch the keyhole with your horn.

Thank you so much, Great Vurnerrah! I am so honored to have conversed with you!"

Before I could protest that I'd not really talked, she gave a quick curtsey and was off. I waited until she was out of sight before letting out a long breath. She was exhausting, but I liked her.

I also liked having access to the convent and its forests. I took down a large, lazy, fattened elk and gorged myself. I wouldn't have to eat for days, a feeling I'd almost forgotten. Then I washed off in a nearby stream and slaked my thirst. I still had enough time to snag a couple of rabbits for the sisters before returning. Touching my horn to the keyhole did indeed work, and I was able to drop my offering to the sisters before settling into one of the back pews just as the bells rang to announce Compline.

The sisters filed in, Grace among them. They took their places in a small half-circle before the altar. After the short prayer, Mother Superior called for an examination of conscience. I got so caught up cataloging my list of sins that I almost missed it when she instructed Sister Grace to lead the psalm.

There was a pause. I could not see Grace's face, but even in the back, I could feel the spike of adrenaline and fear that surged through her. But the sisters, led by their mother superior, waited patiently.

The silence stretched, broken only by Grace's ragged breathing.

Mother Superior nodded, not so much in encouragement but as if to remind her of her cue.

And Grace sang.

Her voice was tentative and breathy—yet the words and the notes flowed from her mouth as if she sang them every day. The sisters joined in as if it were nothing out of the ordinary, and their calm seemed to comfort her, because her voice grew stronger.

Around them, magic swirled in its own dance of protectiveness and praise.

After, the sisters filed out, but Grace peeled off the line and sat on the front pew as if too weak to move on. Hands in her lap, she bowed her head. I would have thought her praying if she didn't seem to be curled in on herself. I started toward her, but Mother Superior took a seat beside her.

"Do you understand now?" she asked Grace in a hushed voice. "All these years, Satan's forces have caused you to deny God the gift of your voice. Today, you snatched that victory from them. But this is your fight, now—now and every day. You are called to this battle."

Grace nodded. Then she fell against Mother Superior and sobbed into her shoulder.

I decided to make a discreet exit.

Chapter Ten: Unconventional Respite

The convent bells rang way too early. I growled quietly as I rotated so my head faced away from the window. I adjusted a wrinkle in the braided rug before draping my tail over my eyes to cut out the not-yet-light of dawn.

"Are ye so spoiled by the Mundane world, then?" the sleepy voice of Sister Grace teased from the bed.

"I'm a dragon," I retorted. "When I want to praise God, I launch myself into the air in the brightness of the day to dance among the clouds. Rising at ridiculous hours to worship in a tiny, cold room together is a custom developed by masochistic mortals."

"Mmm," Grace murmured as she rose from bed. She stretched. "And how well did that excuse work with the Pope?"

Grumbling under my breath about uppity nuns with far too much wit, I got up and joined her.

Protests aside, I did enjoy early morning prayers. The chapel, though too cool for my tastes in the late October chill, was nonetheless cozy from the love and joy the sisters put into their worship. The stained-glass windows filtered the sunrise, dappling the sisters in light of blue, gold, and red. The ambient magic that hung thick and expectant elsewhere seemed to sway and sparkle, as if reflecting grace. And speaking of... Sister Grace again sang, and her voice was stronger this morning. I had a sense of the power and beauty it must have once commanded. Mother Superior was right—a great evil was done by denying God that gift. God—and the world— and me. I resolved to find ways to get her to sing more often.

After, the sisters left for breakfast, and Sister Grace filed out with them. I followed. I was still full of elk, but I was not going to turn down free food. My stomach could handle it. Besides, even though Grace seemed more confident, I wanted to be sure she didn't fall into the shakes once we got out of the comforting confines of the chapel. But, while quiet, she didn't seem nearly as upset as last night. I supposed I shouldn't have been surprised. Dragons don't cry, but I'd seen the positive effect a good long bawl has on mortals.

Still, when one of the sisters sat opposite us and introduced herself as "Sister Lucy, the Choirmaster," I sensed the tightening of Grace's muscles under her habit. However, she greeted her sweetly enough. We bowed our heads as Mother Superior led grace, then dug in.

After a few bites of her oatmeal, Sister Lucy said, "I've been released from my duties today so that I can work with you."

"On the song?" Grace glanced up sharply, her question full of trepidation and hope. I think she expected that the sisters would discount her as everyone else had or that they'd simply take over.

But Sister Lucy cocked her head. "Song? Oh! The one you brought for us to study? I'm afraid that if I'm not allowed to sing it, I wouldn't be much help in deciphering its meaning. No, I've been asked to coach you on your singing."

Grace dropped her spoon.

Mistaking her fear for insult or shyness, Sister Lucy hastened to reassure her. She reached out and grasped Grace's wrist. "You have a beautiful voice! And it's obvious you've had serious training. You're just out of practice, is all. Mother Superior said you've not sung in...years?"

Grace nodded. "I...couldn't. I'm not sure that I..."

I set my paw on her other hand. "You don't have to sing any spells. Right, Sister Lucy?"

"Spells?" She laughed in surprise. "Heavens, no! I was thinking scales, simple exercises, some standard chants. Things to help you regain your range and tone. Nothing too involved."

I cocked my head at Grace beguilingly. "There's no magic in bunch of scales, right?"

"I suppose not." Shrugging out of both our grips, she picked up her spoon and resumed eating.

She asked me to accompany them, and I agreed, just in case there was a spell in a bunch of scales. Besides, I didn't have anything better to do. I spent the morning in a sunny corner of the music room listening to Grace do-re-mi in a multitude of keys before moving to the Psalms in different chant styles. As the hours passed without any magical sparks, Grace began to relax and even enjoy herself.

The next day passed in the same way—prayers, simple meals, song—but after breakfast on the third day, Mother Superior pulled Grace and me aside. She led us to her office, a small and crowded room with shelves full of old books, scrolls, and artifacts religious and otherwise. A narrow table lined one wall. It held vials and bottles of liquids of varying colors and thicknesses, and a Bunsen burner—a Mundane device that was gaining popularity among potion makers in the Faerie realm. The room even smelled crowded, a combination of dust and herbs, oils and potions, the acrid scent of burner fuel, and the earthy smell of aged but cared-for furniture.

Mother Superior settled herself on the tall chair in front of her lab table and indicated for Grace to take the more comfortable guest chair. I settled myself on my haunches and tucked my tail around me so I wouldn't smack it against a pile of papers.

"It seems that you are correct. There is syntax to 'Mishmash.' It would help if we knew the pronunciation and inflections."

"I could get you a recording," I offered.

"You don't want a recording of that song," Grace insisted. "Not here."

Mother Superior held up her hand in a plea for patience. "It need not be of the song itself, just the pronunciation of certain words. There's no need to sing them, either. We can assign the proper notes and tones as written in the music. Is there a Mundane you could ask, someone away from the Gap who is familiar with the song? As I understand it, it's very popular in the Unified States."

"United States," I corrected. "And yeah. It's what they call an earworm."

Mother Superior laughed. "What a delightful and disgusting turn of phrase. What Mundanes lack in magic, they certainly make up for in other ways."

Grace wasn't seeing anything delightful at the moment. She pulled at the edge of her sleeves. "You shouldn't have any recording. That song should not be vocalized at all."

"We would take every precaution," Mother Superior said reassuringly, but when Grace did not look up, she sighed. "However, I will acquiesce to your judgment. You have had the most first-hand experience with this song, and you were the first to see the malignancy where no one else had. We'll keep studying. But there may come a point where we need those verbalizations in order to create a counterspell; you do understand that?"

Grace nodded. She looked like she might cry.

Mother Superior hopped off her chair and patted her on the shoulder. "We can cross that bridge when we get to it. Now, Sister Lucy says you've made great strides with your singing. Do you think you would be comfortable to sing at Mass with us?"

"Aye. Aye, I would like that! Thank you, Mother Superior."

Crowded as the office was, there was still plenty of room for the joy that radiated from Sister Grace.

The next few days went well. Grace felt confident enough that I didn't need to stand guard over her practice sessions, though I did sit in for a few to enjoy her voice. I didn't say anything so as not to scare her, but there was a magic being captured in her singing. It was the magic found in the best of worship, however; the kind that draws others into the ecstasy of beholding Truth.

Once upon a time, dragons had had that kind of magic. We lost it when our eldestkin decided it wasn't enough. Nestled on a center pew where the acoustics were perfect, and Grace's voice seemed to swirl about me as she sang Eldon's Ave Maria, I wondered if we'd ever recapture that magic again. If I'd ever wield that kind of magic again.

I shook myself. God's will—and God's time. I was an immortal being. I could afford to wait. In the meantime, God had called me to other work, and if that meant babysitting an angsty nun, well, I'd had worse assignments.

Besides, it was more like a vacation. Listen to Grace sing, hunt in the woods, hang out with Sister Fangirl and soak in her effusive praise... I could gladly do this for a month or twenty.

But all good things come to an end, and when dealing with mortal beings, that end often came sooner than I liked.

I was lazing by the gates enjoying the midday sun and getting my cheek crests and my ego stroked by Sister Hero Worship when the gate bell rang. She jumped up and hurried to the peephole door. She gave a small "oh!" of surprise, but instead of fleeing like she had with Sister Grace and me, she moved her hands in a spell, then opened the gate to admit the visitor.

A young man in the herald's dress of the Duchy of Peebles-on-Tweed entered, leading his horse who was also adorned in official heraldry. He was a gangly one, maybe 17, with runner's legs and sinewy muscles. I could pick my teeth with his elbow. His nose was crooked and too long for his narrow face. My first thought was that I'd have to fatten him up before he'd make even a snack, but there was something familiar about the shape of his eyes and the shock of red hair.

He looked at me, blanched slightly, and straightened his shoulders. "Vern d'Wyvern, currently of the Mundane but under the lordship of the Diocese of Peeblesford and the Duchy of Peebles-on-Tweed. I bear a message and command from the Seneschal of Peebles-on-Tweed."

"Command, huh?" I looked him over, sniffed. There was something distantly familiar about him. "Do I know you?"

He swallowed but met my eyes. I gave him points for moxie. "You set my grandfather on fire."

I sat back, pleased as the memory clicked. "That's it. I knew you were familiar. How is Herald Gerald?"

"Still cursing your name."

I burst out laughing. Moxie, indeed! Sister Disillusioned was staring at me, shocked. I shrugged. "When a dragon is ignoring you, you should not try to get his attention by using a pitchfork."

Truth was, I'd been in a bad place back then, battling my own inner demons left over from the war. The last thing I'd wanted to do was attend some party of the duke's so he could brag about housing Faerie's sole dragon. Instead, I did a treasureload of penance. The biggest insult of it was, I didn't even breathe fire on Gerald. I smacked him with my tail, and he fell into a lantern.

The boy continued, "Grandfather has retired. I am Charlie Wilmot, son of Senior Herald Charles Wilmot."

Ah, yes, Herald Wilmot, who delivered the message to the President of the United States that if it wanted to maintain friendly relations with Faerie, the Mundane was going to have to keep the dragon that the duke had formerly been so proud of hosting. "I'll make you a deal: You don't hold Grandpa against me, and I won't hold Pa against you. So what's the message?"

I didn't think the kid could get more ramrod straight, but he managed. With eyes staring ahead as if making a proclamation to the crowd, he announced, "Vern d'Wyvern, currently of the Mundane but under the lordship..."

"Yes, yes," I interrupted. "I got that part. "Relax, take a breath, and tell me what they want. Paraphrase."

He paused, blinking, and I realized then that he was using his officiousness as a shield. So, I was going to like this even less than I'd liked his grandfather's invitation to be the duke's *objet de curiosité*. I sighed. "I won't kill the messenger. Or dismember him. Or harm him in any way. I'll stay calm. I promise."

With a long expulsion of air, Charlie seemed to deflate from his over-tense bearing into something more suiting a teenage Faerie human. "You've been recalled to Los Lagos for questioning. Apparently, you helped a suspected criminal escape the Mundane?"

I was glad that I had made my promise to keep my temper. It made it that much more fun to watch Sister Grace lose hers.

Upon Charlie's declaration, Sister Eloise had run for Mother Superior and Sister Grace. Poor discomfited Charlie had had to cool his heels until they arrived, then repeat his message all over again.

"Helped me *escape*?" she yelled, and Herald Charlie flinched. "I left the Mundane on my own, thank ye very much—and no one had a problem with it then."

"Don't kill the messenger," I warned, trying not to grin too hard.

Charlie, however, seemed better with humans than dragons. "Begging your pardon, sister, but according to the police authorities of Los Lagos, Sister Grace McCarthy was remanded to the custody of Vern D'Wyvern of DragonEye, PI."

"Oh, I was, was I?" She turned her glare of Irish fire at me. "So, that's why you've been hanging out with me, then?"

Charlie cocked his head. "No one's said anything about hanging, mum."

"No one said anything about 'custody,' either," Grace said to me.

"I would have, but you'd already escaped to Faerie," I said. I turned to Charlie. "I didn't have anything to do with aiding and abetting a suspect."

Charlie shrugged. He was the messenger, not the judge.

"I didn't escape, and I didn't do anything wrong," she repeated.

"You compelled a child to stop singing," I countered.

"I stopped a child from singing one song. A song that isn't even a song but was some kind of summoning or transformation. I don't know—

and I wasn't going to let her finish to find out. If I'd pulled a child out of the way of a speeding car, would I be culpable if that child scraped a knee?"

"Well, actually..." I shrugged. Mundanes had "good Samaritan" laws, and yet, people still sued those who came to their rescue.

Her eyes narrowed as she took in my meaning. "You're joking."

I gave her my most innocent, helpless looks. Charlie, meanwhile, was muttering that he'd love to see a real Mundane car. Sister Former Fangirl was watching the two of us argue, unsure whose side to take, and Mother Superior kept her gaze on Sister Grace. I didn't think the argument was what interested her so much as Grace's reaction. Sister Grace was red-faced with fury, and yet the magic that surrounded her was not gathering into a storm nor rushing about her in protective reaction. I'd noticed it, too. Even though she refused to wield magic, she was again regaining control over it.

Good thing, too. Otherwise, she might have worked some St. George-level hurt on my scaley hide.

Instead, she took a deep, cleansing breath, and started counting to ten—a Mundane trick for regaining one's temper, though she adapted it to "One Hail Mary, Two Hail Mary." At Six Hail Mary, she gave up. "All right then. Let's go. Ye best be turning me in."

I laughed in disbelief. "And admit I was guilty? I don't think so. I did not help you escape—you went home after telling me you were going to make things right with Santry. I thought I was off the hook being your babysitter."

"Babysitter? Is that what you've been doing this whole time, babysitting the crazy nun?"

Both Charlie and Sister Eloise backed up a step. Mother Superior gathered them up like ducklings and ushered them to the building, leaving Grace and me to finish our discussion.

"You're not crazy," I told her. "You're just—"

"Just what?"

"Just too timid to take care of yourself or anyone else!" I half-shouted. "You can tell yourself you were saving that child all you want, and maybe you did, but I don't think you ever meant to do that. I think you got scared and acted on reflex. Did you know you cast that spell?"

"I..."

I didn't let her finish, lest she say a lie she'd have to confess later. "Of course you didn't. You lost control. For all the best reasons, maybe, but not in a conscious decision. That's why you let Santry arrest you instead of appealing to Bishop Aiden or your order. And that's why you came here instead of to your own mother-house."

"My mother-house didn't believe me."

"You have more evidence now. No. You were afraid they'd lock you up again. Put you in a sleeping spell for a hundred years and try again later."

"How did you...?"

"I'm good at my job. But you're not getting shoved away again—not by them, not by the Mundanes. Not while you're under *my* protection."

She stood a moment, shaking with emotion. I didn't know if she was going to insist on giving into her fears and sacrificing herself for what those fears told her was the greater good, or if she'd yell at me some more for being such a presumptuous drake.

Instead, she clasped her hands over her cross. She nodded. "Okay. What do you suggest?"

Her trust filled my heart with warmth, but I didn't let it show. I was not ready to admit that we were friends. "I'll go back to the Mundane. I'll tell Santry you had already left, and I was tracking you down. It's not even a lie."

She nodded, still tense. "And if he asks if you know where I am?"

"I'll tell him I know where you were when I got called back to the Mundane."

Now, she broke into a sly grin. "And you'll be sounding most annoyed, will ye not? You're very good at this."

"I've had practice. In the meantime, you stay here. Work on your singing—and your relationship with magic. If you never want to cast a spell again in your life, fine—but you'd better be sure you don't do so by accident."

She looked at the ground, ashamed. "I... I don't deserve your kindness."

I reached out with a claw and gently made her meet my gaze. "You'll pay me back later," I told her.

Chapter Eleven: Nunthing to Report

I debated taking a detour to see Bishop Aiden on the way back, but since he'd decided to let his dear brother, the duke, handle my recall, I decided he wasn't worth my attention. Besides, Charlie knew exactly where to find me, which meant Aiden had known all along where we were, and probably had a good idea of what we were doing. If he had any important information for me, he'd have sent it to the convent.

Charlie escorted me to the Gap, which on this side did not have a large, clean, and highly bureaucratized port of entry, but a cobblestone road leading to a loosely guarded entrance. Scattered about were tents and a few permanent buildings all professing to carry Genuine Faerie Artifacts™. Many claimed to be magic; somewhat fewer actually were. It was a nice day, not too chilly, so most of the tourists coming through were making detours to window shop.

There were a few beggars lounging in the corners, hoping to get their last coppers before the winter storms drove them to other pursuits. I paused before one who sat slumped, lame, and misshapen, against the edge of one of the larger stores. He appeared to have lost one leg below the knee. He had a sign written in perfect Mundane English: *Leg eaten by dragon. Please Help. God bless.*

I tapped Charlie on the shoulder with my tail and we moseyed over to the man. His face went pale. A pretty convincing display of fear, and probably a real one, if for the wrong reasons.

I set a long claw on his sign and pulled it toward me. "That's funny. I don't remember biting you."

"It was... another dragon," he said, his voice shaking.

"There aren't any other dragons," I replied, my voice probably taking on the same tone that Grace had used when telling Addison to stop being an annoying little brat. For a moment, I fancied what it would be like to channel magic through that tone.

"Yes, there are!" he cried, too quickly and too desperately.

I didn't bother arguing with him. We both knew the truth, and the streets were empty of tourists at the moment. Instead, I leaned in close. "Are you tasty?"

He scrambled up on two good legs and ran for the hills.

Charlie buckled over laughing. "Bravo, Vern!"

At the gate, Charlie paused to tell the guard about the beggar and to inform him the duke would not stand for someone spreading such heinous lies about Faerie folk. Even though Charlie was barely a man, he wore the heraldry of the duke, and that wielded authority. The guard swallowed visibly and promised they'd make sure the beggar had a less slanderous placard next time.

Charlie nodded approval. We took a few steps into the open area before the Gap. He looked longingly at the large, roughly circular gateway. It was singularly plain to those who can't see magic, but I knew he was looking past to the wonders beyond.

"Well," he said. "I suppose this is farewell for now."

"I don't think so," I replied. "You did go all the way to Stanshire-on-Tweed to fetch me. The least you can do is escort me all the way to police headquarters."

"Truly?" His voice cracked with excitement. Then he cleared it and said, forcing himself to speak deeply and authoritatively. "Quite so. It would be the most conscientious action to take."

"Wouldn't want you to be derelict in your duties," I agreed.

Charlie managed to maintain his composure as we crossed the gate. He kept from gaping at the Mundane port, with its huge plate-glass windows, steel framework, and shiny terrazzo flooring. He refrained from asking to ride the escalator twice, although I knew he wanted to. He even acted completely casual as I went to the transportation desk and got us a car to take us to the police station.

As we waited for the car, a woman approached us, fury in her eyes. "What kind of monstrosity is this?"

For a moment, I thought she meant me, but she was pointing at Charlie. Naturally, the lime-green tunic under a Halloween orange tabard was bad enough, but her horrified expression seemed reserved for the bloody boar's head on a pike that sat over a quartered field of alternating lime green and blue.

"I wear the heraldry of the Duchy of Peebles-on-Tweed," he said.

"It's a severed head! You think it's cool to wear the torn head of a pig? The poor innocent animal."

"Innocent? My lady, you've been misinformed. This is the head of Borazoron the Terrible, no ordinary swine but a boar of incredible size and ferocity. He terrorized the fields and forests of Peebles-on-Tweed. He and his pack of feral boars destroyed farms, razed villages, killed children. 'Twas the first Duke of Peebles-on-Tweed who killed the beast, and his heraldry stands today as his promise to protect the people and the land, no matter how fearful the foe."

"Oh," she paused, non-plussed, then rallied. "Well, still, that's no reason to be so violent about it. He should have killed the animal humanely or released it to somewhere away from people."

"But my lady, Borazoron was possessed by the devil himself."

She scoffed. "I don't believe in the devil."

"You would have had you looked into his eyes or seen the steam rise off its body, fetid and vile against the clean autumn air. Many a shining knight tried to give Borazoron a clean death, but the boar never returned the favor. The king lost a legion of his best men before putting out a call…"

Charlie wove the story of how the duke's ancestor, a rough but wily woodsman, tracked and fought the boar. As he described the epic battle, people paused in their coming and going to listen. Even his vegan heckler was spellcast, so to speak. Oration is still a common skill in Faerie, but Charlie had a natural flair for it.

"…and so, brave Davon, bleeding, bruised, yet victorious, dragged himself and his prize back to the palace. With the last of his strength, he thrust the pike with the severed head of Borazoron before the throne…and collapsed."

"Did he die?" whispered our antagonizer, and for a moment, I thought she might actually shed a tear for the pig-murderer.

"Nay, my lady. Davon was as stout of body as he was of heart. The king's own physician, aided by a Sister of Our Lady of Miracles, healed him of the many gores and gory wounds, and then he was given the lands of Peebles-on-Tweed as his own. To this day, his progeny stand ready to protect the duchy from all threats."

"What? He didn't get to marry a princess?" Some teenage boy wearing dark, torn clothes and a matching sneer asked.

Charlie regarded him as if he were a lord himself. "Nay. Davon was as humble as he was strong. He knew the life of royalty was not for him, and that the fair princess deserved someone of better manners than his rough ways. No, he married Lady Sally Witherspoon, a lass nubile and fertile, and they had seven sons and eight daughters."

The crowd broke up then, our vegan tsking under her breath about the irresponsibility of having 15 kids. There's no pleasing some people. Some of our audience tried to pay Charlie for his story, which he refused, but I graciously accepted on his behalf. If nothing else, I could tip the driver who waited so patiently for us.

Once in the SUV, Charlie could no longer contain himself and transformed from herald to tourist. "This is amazing!" he exclaimed as he scanned the interior of the car. He leaned toward the driver, taking in the controls hungrily. "How fast can it go?"

Apparently, our driver was used to "newfies" as first-time visitors to the Mundane were called. "I don't go past 80," he said, laughing, as he eased Charlie back to his seat, explained the seatbelt, and started the car.

Meanwhile, I translated 80 into Faerie speeds.

"Bloody hell! Can I try?"

After we were on the highway and he got a chance to marvel at the trees and mile markers whizzing by, Charlie calmed down and started asking more serious questions. He opened the glovebox and pulled out the manual.

"Can you read that?" the driver asked.

"Aye. I'm very good at languages. I'm fluent in M'English, Common, Latin, Grit—"

"That's the trade language of the dwarves," I explained. I figured the driver already knew that M'English meant English as spoken in the Mundane.

Charlie continued, his eyes scanning the book as he spoke. "I know some phrases of the Eternal Winds tribes, and a smattering of Fairy Court. And I'd like to learn M'Espanol. I hear that's a popular language here."

Our driver whistled. "I know some Spanish—M'Espanol—but I've never been good at it."

"I have to be if I want to be the duke's agent in the Mundane as well as Faerie. What's a 'variable transmission'? Do you send messages through the car?"

By the time we pulled up in front of the police station, our driver had given Charlie a crash course (no pun intended) on cars, driving, and cell phone technology. I wondered if he had a prepared lecture. I'm sure he heard these questions all the time, although I suspected Charlie's were probably more intelligent and in-depth. I was growing to like this kid. He had a bright future, not like his klutzy grandfather.

Inside, the desk sergeant buzzed us in. It was a quiet afternoon apparently, with most people catching up on paperwork and one officer booking a prostitute. She looked up when we stepped in, and wolf whistled at Charlie.

Vialpando spun in his chair and almost spat out his coffee when he saw Charlie. "Whoa! What the f—"

I cut him off. "Santry paged me."

I don't think he got the pun, but he chortled, anyway and jerked a thumb toward the office. "He's in. Rhodes," he called to an officer at a nearby desk, "ring the captain and let him know."

"Will do," she replied cheerily, then as we passed said, *soto voce*, "Nice outfit."

Charlie was indeed fluent in many languages, including sarcasm. For the first time, I saw him blush.

Santry, of course, regarded us with the same expression he usually wore: tired and slightly annoyed. He did raise a skeptical brow Charlie's way, but all he said was, "You're the herald they sent to retrieve Vern?"

"He made quick work of it, too," I answered.

"And Sister Grace?"

"That will take somewhat longer," I replied, which was true if not totally honest.

Santry leaned back in his seat and crossed his arms, still staring at Charlie.

Charlie straightened as he would when addressing the Seneschal. "I thought it best to deliver the one I could manage to retrieve, sir," he said, his eyes at that thousand-yard stare of any official lackey who was defending himself when being dressed down by a superior officer.

"Do you even shave yet?" Santry asked.

Charlie's face colored slightly, but he didn't rise to the bait.

Santry let him stew a minute longer, but when Charlie didn't break, told Vialpando to take him outside and show him the precinct. "Introduce him around, too."

"I'm a babysitter?" Vialpando griped.

"You're an orientation officer. If he's going to be the rep to the Mundane, he should know how we do things."

Vialpando started to protest, then turned thoughtful. "Hm. Yeah. Okay. Let's go, kid."

"That's Herald Wilmot," Charlie corrected. He didn't move.

"You heard the herald," Santry said, and made a shooing motion toward the door.

Vialpando opened the door and made an exaggerated, sweeping bow. "Of course, your lordship."

Charlie bowed toward Santry and left. As he passed Vialpando, he said, "Heralds are not lords. Perhaps you need an orientation, too."

Santry let the door shut and waited until the two had walked further into the bullpen before dropping his stern posture. He relaxed—as much as Santry ever relaxes—and shook his head. "He's a child. He should be playing video games or something."

"No video technology in Faerie. And seventeen is a lot older over there, especially when you're carrying on a legacy. Charlie takes his responsibilities seriously," I replied. With my peripheral vision, I tracked Charlie and Vialpando through Santry's glass wall. In the bullpen, a small crowd had gathered around the pair. They seemed to be part asking questions and part mocking his dress. He was taking it in stride. Good.

Santry had this weird philosophy about hazing. He considered it training for the abuse his officers could likely face when dealing with the criminal element—or the entitled or bigoted citizen who didn't like policemen in general or one of his people in particular. His officers were ruthless to the newbies, but also equally ruthless when protecting them in the field from similar abuse. It was a weird dynamic that worked for those who could put up with it long enough to 'graduate.' They were a tough, tight-knit group that kept their cool when the public got nasty. Even Vialpando, except when it came to me.

I guess since I "freelance," I'll never graduate in his mind.

The fact that Santry had left Charlie to Vialpando's "tender mercies" meant he expected to see more with the Faerie herald in the future—and was okay with that.

"Speaking of responsibilities, do you not remember that I made you responsible for watching Sister Grace?" Santry accused.

"That would have been a lot easier if you had ordered her not to leave town," I accused back. "I followed her to Faerie. Check with the GSA if you don't believe me."

A movement caught my attention. In the bull-pen, the teasing had gotten serious. The circle around Charlie had widened as people took a step back. Vialpando was tapping his chest: *Come at me, bro.*

Santry, even though he had a better view than I did, pretended not to notice. "Do you know where she is?"

If he wasn't worried, I certainly wasn't. I pretended not to watch as Charlie feigned a swing, ducked under Vialpando's response, and lunged again with his knife before you could say, "your lordship." Vialpando leapt back with a quiet yelp I could nonetheless hear. But everyone could hear his cry of alarm when he stumbled on a chair and fell backward. Charlie moved in, then jerked back, hands in the air. Vialpando had drawn his sidearm.

"I know where she'd been," I said as Santry's eyes took in the scene among his officers, and, after assuring himself his officer had his hand off the trigger, he dismissed it from his concern. "I know where she was. I also know that she's not trying to run away. She's still investigating that song."

Santry made a fist, and his eyes flared. "That song! It's worse than that beaver song."

"The one that goes…"

"Don't, or I will shoot you."

I held my tongue. Santry was more likely to make good on his threat than Vialpando was to shoot Charlie. Besides, the Billy Beaver theme song was a horrible earworm and as saccharine as the theme park that inspired it.

Meanwhile, the amusements continued in the bullpen. Covering Charlie with his sidearm just to make the point, Vialpando stood up slowly, well out of Charlie's reach. Then he holstered his weapon, preening.

At least until Charlie loosened his fist to reveal the bottom half of Vialpando's tie.

As Vialpando gaped and sputtered at his sliced necktie—which apparently, was a favorite, ugly as it was—the rest of the crowd laughed and cheered.

The edge of Santry's face quirked upward, which was as much approval as he was going to display. He continued our conversation as if nothing were happening outside the windows of his office.

"I would not be surprised to learn that song is evil. It gave me the creeps like no song has ever done. Even so, much as I'd like to make everyone stop singing that abomination of tempo and mixolydian mode, we can't have nuns hexing away free will."

Now it was my turn to get angry. "Listen, Santry. Grace didn't hex anyone. She can't. Literally. That kind of spell would not work. She's a nun. Consecrated. A worker of holy magics."

"What about natural magics?" he pressed.

"Look at you doing your homework." I smirked. Meanwhile, I saw that Charlie had given Vialpando the other half of his tie. Someone else handed him a stapler. Vialpando sneered at the officer. Show over, folks started to disperse. Charlie twisted his dagger and presented it to Vialpando, hilt-first, for inspection. Vialpando responded by removing the magazine from his gun, clearing the chamber, and handing it to Charlie. Yeah, that kid was going to go far.

Of course, I had a better poker face than Santry, so for all he knew, I was oblivious to the scene going on between his officer and my herald.

I continued, "No. She can work natural magics—or could, if she would let herself. Any mage, consecrated, unholy, or secular can work natural magics. But a consecrated mage isn't like a secular mage who still has the capacity for maliciousness. For Grace to do harmful magic would take serious long-term effort on her part. She'd have to damage her soul first."

"Are you sure she's not damaged?" There was something gentle about his tone that made me stop and consider.

"Damaged? Maybe, her psyche. But not her soul. And not evil. I'd know. And if I thought she was turning to the Dark Side, I wouldn't bring her to you, anyway. I'd have already taken her to the authorities on Faerie."

I thought I was going to have to explain, but Santry nodded. "Okay, then. Is there anything to that song?"

"I won't know unless you let me go back to Faerie and find out," I said. "I know she delivered a copy to her order. I was at the convent, following up, when Charlie found me."

Santry sighed. For all that we didn't get along, I knew he was an intelligent being. He knew I wasn't telling the entire truth. "Do her sisters believe her, then?"

"Enough to devote some serious resources to the research."

By his desk, the crowd now dispersed, Vialpando was patting Charlie on the shoulder. He led him away toward the hall that led to the shooting range.

Looks like Charlie graduated. That had to be a record.

Santry rubbed his forehead, a sure sign he was going to do something he suspected he'd regret later. "This Addison hexing scandal is getting out of hand." He held up a hand to forestall my protest. "I know. But what you don't know is that your bishop brought in a Faerie mage to assess Addison—and she started flopping on the ground as soon as he tried to touch her. He'd like to speak to Sister Grace. Personally, I think this isn't going to get better unless that child has a sudden reversal. If you go back to Faerie and find Sister Grace, I expect you to bring her to me. Do you understand?"

I got what he meant, but I didn't understand. "Why are you being so nice to her?"

He met my skeptical gaze with one of cold ice. "I'm not nice."

Then he turned back to his computer. "I am, however, just. You might check with your friend, Father Rich, and find out what you've missed while you were boondoggling in Faerie. Come back in an hour for the kid—sorry, the *herald*."

Chapter Twelve: Hell on Feelz

I decided to check on my place before heading over to Little Flower. It was Father Rich's day off, so with any luck I could happen by just in time for dinner. What I saw when I got home ruined my appetite, however.

My place isn't much to begin with. Even so, that didn't mean I wasn't furious at the vandalism done in my absence. The doghouse was smashed, and the dogs gone—escaped through the hole cut in my fence or carried off to a shelter. The walls and windows of my already ugly home were defaced with anti-dragon and anti-Faerie slurs. The yard stank of urine—not from animals, but from humans who apparently didn't understand how my species or their own marked territory.

That was just another sign that this was not the work of ordinary vandals taking advantage of my absence. I had come to an understanding with the local hoodlums after I'd put the Fear of Vern into them. They were surprisingly smart kids; I hadn't even had to eat any of them to make my point. The people who did this, however, played at intelligence without actually being wise.

Revelation 13. I sighed at the reference. It always got on my nerves. Honestly, do I have seven heads and ten horns? It was a blasphemy of a dragon, which was the point. Evil twists the good into something grotesque, like the traditional demon with a faun's shape, but red skin and a barbed tail. But do humans hate Narnia because of Tumnus? Of course not. Or consider snakes. I've yet to see a holy war against the slithering species, even though Satan took their form to tempt Eve. For that matter, Satan is always taking human form. Do other creatures think every man is a demon because he's a biped? No, it's us poor dragons that are stuck living down an undeserved reputation just because a demon sort-of-took our form in John's vision. Or rather, I had to, since I was the only dragon left and thus the only one who had to deal with Mundanes, who alone of all the species in God's universe were unable to count heads.

Unfortunately, it was too cold for whitewashing, even if I had the time, and if I tried to burn it off, I'd probably set fire to my stupid house, which, dismal as it was, was nonetheless a roof over my head and relative protection from the elements...and less trouble than living in the parish's garage. With a sigh of resignation, I opened the torn screen door and made my way inside.

A window was broken, and the place was freezing. Fortunately, it had not snowed during my absence. All my electronics were still in their place, too. I wondered if Los Despredatores had anything to do with that. I'd made it clear that I'd consider them responsible if my stuff was ever stolen. Nah, more likely, none of my genteel vandals had wanted to brave entering the dragon's den. Alas, that meant no one had availed themselves of the cheap dreck the previous owner had left in the stacks of cardboard boxes that crowded my home.

I did a quick circuit of the place just to be sure I didn't miss anything that might bite me in the tail later, and, having satisfied myself that the protestors had satisfied *themselves* with rude language and inappropriate use of Biblical references, I went to address the window. A human would have taped cardboard to it while cursing their fate. But I was a dragon.

The glass lay on the floor, along with the offending rock. Most of the pieces had broken clean. Good. A few minutes of playing jigsaw, and I had the pieces on a cookie sheet in the approximate shape of the hole. With some targeted fire breathing, I fused them to one piece and put it into the hole. With a little more fire breathing and some fidgeting, I then melted the glass to seal the cracks.

The result was warped and messy. Fortunately, I don't have a view outside my window to ruin.

I cursed my fate.

Calling the shelters in a fruitless search for my dogs and putting the rest of my place in order took more than an hour. Fortunately, when I called the station, I discovered that some of the officers had taken Herald Charlie under their wing and were treating him to dinner and a ride-along. My young charge taken care of, I headed over to the Little Flower rectory, flying high and avoiding areas where people might be outdoors. Why ask for trouble, when I had enough already? Fortunately, the cold air encouraged people to stay cozy indoors. I was looking forward to joining them.

When I got to the parish parking lot, I saw a familiar car in the extra clergy slot. What was Father Rich's sister doing here? Her Texas assignment was supposed to last another year. If he had had to call in the reinforcements, things were worse than I thought. Not to mention, dinner would be whatever low-fat entre Bernadette decided her brother needed—and certainly not enough to satisfy a dragon's appetite. That's what I got for not calling ahead.

With a sigh of resignation—something I seemed to be doing a lot this afternoon—I landed on the porch and rang the doorbell.

Father opened it. "'Bout time," was his only comment as he let me in.

"Santry warned you I was coming?" I guessed. "I had to check my place first. The Anti-Faerie movement seems to be enjoying themselves." I summarized the damage to my place and my re-pairs.

"Smart idea," Father said as we entered the dining room. It was set for four. "We're expecting sleet tonight," he concluded before I could ask who else was eating with us.

"Joy."

"That's what I said." Bernadette emerged from the kitchen, a bowl of pasta in her hands. Or what she called pasta, which was really some kind of stringy squash and veggies in a tomato sauce. Not that it tasted bad, mind you, but I was glad for the elk I'd eaten the day before.

Behind her, carrying a platter with two store-bought roast chickens, was a priest in a black cassock with a thin piping of dark blue—the same color as Grace's habit. Behind his beard, I caught the red trim of his priest's collar. So Aiden had sent a mage of the Inquisition to check Addison's story? Had he been that worried, or was he hoping to impress the Mundanes? If the latter, I needed to have a talk with him about Mundane attitudes.

Father introduced us, and we sat down at the table. After prayers and passing of the pseudo-pasta, I asked, "Are you the priest who had the unfortunate duty of interviewing Addison Lukas?"

The priest smiled ruefully. "If you could call it that. I had barely introduced myself when she went into her fit. I was rushed out and told not to return."

"Which is just what she wanted. She's an expert manipulator for one so young," I said.

Father Raul shrugged. "Some are born with the gift. It can be used for good as well as mischief. She's also an accomplished thespian. I thought she had a medical condition."

Bernadette took two of the drumsticks. I wondered if she really liked them that much or was just trying to make it easier for her brother to choose the less greasy breasts. "Addison's only 'condition' is Oppositional Defiance Disorder coupled with narcissism."

"Brat," I translated for Father Raul.

"Be that as it may," Father Rich said, accepting the slice of skinless chicken breast his sister offered, "Addison and her parents have stirred up a lot of trouble. It's probably a good thing you took Sister Grace to Faerie when you found her."

"How is she?" Father Raul asked. "I would like to interview her as well."

"I don't recall saying I'd found her," I said. Father Rich nodded, understanding my meaning.

"I'll see what I can do," was all I said. I didn't want to reveal where she was—or the fact that all I'd done was follow her and avail myself of a free vacation.

Bernadette continued, "I wish you could do something about Addison. Would you believe she had the gall to demand that she play Mary in the school nativity musical? Despite the fact that she 'can't sing.'" She paused in her eating to make air quotes. "When I refused, her parents complained to the principal. They want her *mother* backstage singing while Addison lip syncs. Sheer ridiculousness aside, how fair is that to the other children? I told them if she wants to be onstage, she can be a camel. I can't even let her be the kings' treasure. They have singing parts."

"You?" I asked. I'd already finished my meal and had to wait to see if the humans wanted seconds before helping myself. "Where's the music teacher?"

"Quit the same day Sister Grace left. She'd gotten it in her head somehow that she was next on Sister Grace's hit list."

"Hit list?" Father Raul asked.

Sister Bernadette explained the idiom. "She thought she'd be the next target. Apparently, she and Sister Grace didn't get along."

The conversation was wrecking my appetite. "For pity's sake. Grace just wanted her to teach songs more appropriate to a Catholic school. And Grace does not have a hit list."

"I'm glad to hear it. Hopefully, we can resolve this situation somehow and she can return. If she wants to. She's not been very well treated. I wouldn't blame her if she never came back."

"It's a misunderstanding fueled by an irascible child and her overly indulgent parents," Father said. "I think it could be better in the long run if she returned. People need to know the Faerie have nothing to hide. Besides, there are children and teachers who miss her. And even among those that don't, most only half believe that Sister Grace took away Addison's ability to sing."

"She didn't," I affirmed. "She prevented her from singing one song—'Mishmash.'"

Father Raul nodded. "A restriction geas, then. That seems straightforward enough."

"Putting spells on children?" Bernadette asked, affronted.

But Father simply shrugged. "It's not unusual for a child to have their abilities restricted until they have the discipline to control them. I didn't realize this Addison had Magical blood. Not that I had a chance to find out, but she seemed fully Mundane."

"She is," I said. "That's what scares Sister Grace." I told him what Grace had told me about seeing tentacles flowing of out and around Addison, while, unaware, she pestered Grace with that song.

Father fell silent then, chewing slowly as he digested my information. I didn't blame him. For an unmagical creature to channel magic meant the magic was using the person, not vice-versa. And to do that, it had to be a pretty powerful spell indeed.

Bernadette, however, scoffed at my story. "Tentacles? Really? I find it hard to imagine that Addison wouldn't have been freaking out if that had happened. Besides, plenty of other people are singing that song. It's abysmal, but catchy. So why aren't we seeing tentacles everywhere?"

"Grace said Addison seemed unaware of what she was doing, like she'd sung herself into a trance," I said. "And the child has perfect pitch. Plus, how many Mundanes, even here in Los Lagos, are going to admit they saw tentacles coming out of someone's mouth?"

"It's like the start of every bad Star Trek episode," Father Rich said. "They'd probably think they were seeing things and dismiss it or be afraid to tell anyone for fear of being thought crazy."

"Or Sister Grace was seeing things," Sister Bernadette said. "I'm sorry. I know she's your friend, but rumors are she was being treated for psychological issues. Occam's Razor: The simplest solution is often the correct one."

A few days ago, I would have sided with her. After all, hadn't I suggested the very thing to Sister Grace? Now, however, I was growing more convinced that something was going on. Plus, for all the evidence I'd seen—the flares of temper, the bottles of pills—I didn't think Grace was crazy. At least not now, and not about this.

As I opened my mouth to argue, Father Rich held up a hand. "Regardless, the fact that this is a common disciplinary tactic is a point in her favor—if, indeed, Addison was prevented from singing a single song."

"But how will you prove it?" Father Raul asked. "I could have done it, but after her performance, I'm not allowed near her. I think we can assume no other mage will be trusted."

"Are you sure it was an act?" Father Rich asked. "She wasn't being influenced by...?" Even as a priest, he couldn't quite make himself say it.

Father Raul, however, had no compunctions. "Demonic possession? I don't think so. Her reaction was more immediate and theatrical than one would expect in such a case. If there was influence, it's very subtle, more of a suggestiveness which would play on her natural tendencies. If I'd been able to touch her, I would have been able to tell; but from a distance, with everyone else's thoughts and emotions so high in reaction to her fit..." He shrugged.

"So we need to prove she's faking it—or at least exaggerating," Father said. "How do we do that?"

"Get her to sing, obviously," his sister said, "but if being Mary in the school musical isn't enough incentive, what is?"

"A bigger audience," I said. "I saw how she lapped up the attention of the cameras."

"The news is no good," Father Rich replied. "She'll want to stage a miracle healing or something instead. It needs to be something more casual, where we can catch her unawares. And I hate to say it, but if we stage it, it'll look like entrapment, and that won't go down very well with the school board."

Sister grunted assent. "So something more casual. Any ideas?"

My phone buzzed with a text. Since another of Sister B's rules was "no phones at the table," I used my tail to have the message played in my ear. It was from Jerry, Junior. *Did I see you fly by? Come over. Addison made Anna cry. We're so sick of her!*

I grinned. "I may have just the thing."

Chapter Thirteen:
Operation Trapison

One thing every Faerie instinctively knows is that sometimes, one species can handle a problem another can't. This applies to adults vs. children as well.

The Costa home was across and down the street from the church, one reason the late Dona Elena decided to blame me for her missing cats. Since her death, the tsunami of tabbies had finally ebbed, thanks to a concerted effort by animal control and the Los Lagos Spay and Neuter Association. Of course, she'd probably still blame me if she were alive.

Fortunately, her nephew was more trusting—and a better judge of character. He opened the door and greeted me with a rueful smile. I understood; I could hear the crying continuing upstairs.

"JJ text you?" he asked.

I shrugged. I wasn't sure exactly how to explain my presence, or my ulterior motive. I did have a suspicion that no matter what I did, it was going to be soggy. "Can I borrow a towel?"

With a chuckle, Jerry, Senior, let me in. He led me up the stairs and ducked into the baby's room to get me a burping rag. I caught a glimpse of Rita trying to nurse the baby, who had obviously picked up on her sister's mood and was fussing. I wondered if she'd called Mrs. Lukas and given her a piece of her mind; she looked pretty frazzled herself.

Well, dragon to the rescue—how ironic was that? Now armed, I entered Anna's room.

I had to hand it to the Costas: the kids stuck together. JJ and Camila were sitting on Anna's bed, rubbing her back as she sobbed into a pillow. Francisco stood guard, but his face had an "I told you so" smirk. Marie was sitting on the floor, playing with a doll.

"We hate Addison!" she announced as I stepped in.

Soon, I had a fifth grader sitting between my paws, bawling into my shoulder while she told me her tale of playground woe, her brothers chiming in their own details and Maria occasionally putting in her two cents trying to spell words that would get her a time out. I wondered which brother had coached her or if her *Phonics Street* videos were starting to show results.

It turned out that Anna had been given the role of Mary in the Christmas musical, since "Miss Pitch Perfect" Addison had been magically muted. ("Which no one believes 'cause she's a lying liar," Frankie clarified.) That was when prima donna Addison showed her true colors, cornering Anna after school to tell her how unworthy she was of the role.

"She told me even if I could sing..." Despite her hiccupy sobs, Anna gave an ugly sneer in imitation of her former friend, "that I was too big and ugly to play a virgin! And, and the only reason I got the part was because I was a... a *suck up!*"

Maria wisely refrained from spelling it this time.

There was more, naturally phrased with Anna being as sweet as she could while Add-evil-son heaped increasing abuse. Knowing both girls, I gave it 75% on the truth meter. Finally, Anna sat back and wiped her eyes on her sleeve. She blew her nose in the damp diaper rag.

"I hate her!" she concluded.

"Now, now," I tsked in that tone that said I was on her side. "Hate isn't what God wants."

Anna pouted, but Frankie yelped in indignation. "He wants us to *love* her?"

I shrugged. "Probably. But I was thinking more about getting justice."

JJ pumped his fist. "I love me some justice! What do we do?"

They all gathered in a circle to listen. Maria even set up her doll to face me and told it to be good. I would have to think about some way to include the ambitious toddler in the plan—or some excuse that she would be better helping elsewhere. I was so not meant for childcare.

I am, however, good at taking care of brats that hurt one of my own.

"First," I said to Frankie, "what did you mean that none of the kids believe her?"

"Randall stands next to her in choir class, and he said he heard her singing when she didn't think anyone was paying attention," Frankie said.

"Randall is not a trustworthy source," I told him.

Undeterred, Frankie continued, "Maybe not, but when he was saying that, some of the other kids were agreeing. Courtney got a weird look on her face, like she wanted to say something but was scared to."

I grinned. I'd been coaching the kids on how to pay attention to their surroundings, especially the people. Jerry, Senior, liked to gripe that I'd make them "grow up weird," but times like this, it paid off. "Does Courtney stand next to her in choir?"

He shook his head. "But maybe she heard her somewhere else? I bet she might tell Anna. She thinks Anna's awesome."

"Awesome!" Maria chimed. "Ah, S U mmm."

"Don't push," I advised Anna. "We don't want to make Addison suspicious and ruin our chance at justice. And is it true what you said the other day that she wants to be a noknok star?"

Noknok—You're There! was the latest social media craze, with a twist. Only group audio or video postings were allowed. The idea, they said, was to inspire people to make art together. "It's about the spirit of cooperation," their ad copy proudly proclaimed. Which, of course, is why Addison was not yet a noknok star. Apparently, her parents had no objection to her starting a channel, but she could not get five other kids to cooperate in giving her the spotlight.

Now, however, I suggested making her dream come true, while ending this nightmare she started.

"But why would she bother? She can't sing—or says she can't, anyway," Jerry, Jr. said.

"You leave that part to me," I said, wondering if Mrs. Lukas ever dreamed of noknok fame. "All you need to do is find about three or four other kids who will play along—and keep a secret. Otherwise, we're all going to be in big trouble."

"We could sing 'Bodalicious.' That was her favorite song before 'Mishmash' came along. It's got a really long high note she loves," Anna suggested. "Bet she can't resist that."

Bouncing and talking excitedly about school tomorrow, the kids followed me down to the kitchen like I was the Pied Piper, which was apt because I'd smelled the pastries when I walked in and was hoping to have a slice of apple before I left. Jerry was just cutting into one as we entered. He took in the faces of his children, now calm and happy, and pursed his lips at me, impressed.

As we all settled down for pie and whipped cream, a half-frozen rain started pattering against the windows.

Rita turned to look at it and tsked. "Don't go out in that, Vern. You can sleep here in the living room tonight."

"Can we have a sleepover? Camila asked.

"No. It's a school night."

"Aw…"

Anna asked, "Papa, can we make a noknok video with Addison? It was Vern's idea."

I tried not to choke on my pie. Way to preemptively throw me under the bus.

"I thought Addison couldn't sing," he said, though his voice expressed doubt and suspicion.

I answered, "We can dub someone in later. Maybe her mom?"

"And autotune it," JJ added, "so no one will know. Please, Dad? It will be fun."

"Addison's really upset about not getting the Mary part," Anna added, her eyes innocent as the

Virgin Mother's. "We just want to give her what she deserves."

"Uh, huh," her father said skeptically. Then he sighed. "All right, then. I don't see why not. But it stays age-appropriate."

"Don't worry," I said. "I'll make sure it's appropriate."

I supposed I should have felt bad about setting up a trap for a ten-year-old child, but Addison started it, and now she'd hurt two ladies I felt compelled to protect. She had it coming.

Besides, Operation Uncover Addison fell together so easily, one could argue that there was some divine influence going on. It turned out, Courtney had heard Addison singing in the girl's room, and when she called Addison on it, was told that if she said anything, not only would Angelic Addison call her a lying liar, but she'd "make sure I had no friends for the rest of my life." She'd said other ugly things, too. Addison obviously watched too many TV shows about high school.

So, we had corroboration: Addison could sing. Check one off the list.

Turned out Courtney's older cousin, a high school junior who wanted to study film, did nok-nok videos with his friends and was only too glad to participate in the setup. I wasn't sure if it was out of brotherly love or if he was seeing an explosion of noks in his future, but Greg seemed to know what he was doing, and he already had a following locally and otherwise. Next check off the list.

It was easy enough to get some kids excited about the video and the chance to get back at Addison, who apparently, was having a bit too much fun with the power the newfound fame that victim status had given her. Frankie and Anna quickly recruited three more kids from their classes who could sing, dance, and take the time for rehearsals...plus had their parents' permission. Check.

Finally, it was up to Anna. By my suggestion, she'd let the hype around the playground build, quietly taking the brunt of Addison's jealousy, until the time was right for a show of humility. The fact that she chose right after a school Mass where Father Rich had preached about forgiveness and turning the other cheek was just a lucky happenstance, I'm sure. They'd assured her that she could lip-sync, and Courtney's cousin would dub her mother's voice in in post-production.

While the kids spent their chilly winter afternoons playing noknok star in a gymnasium with bad acoustics, I tried to clean up both my personal hovel and Territory of the anti-Faerie damage done in my absence. Unfortunately, I could not flame-blast away the slanderous paint job on my house—not unless I wanted to burn down the whole house. I was tempted, mind you; but I didn't have insurance, and even if I did, they'd probably consider me an Act of God and thus exempt themselves from making good on the policy.

There were times while I was out in the fifty-degree weather with a bucket of whitewash and a scrub brush that I considered it, anyway. Might be worth it to have someone officially acknowledge me as God-made and not the devil incarnate. Revelations 13, indeed.

After much too long in the chill, the side of my lair had a sloppy white patch, bright against the dirty beige paint. I was shivering from cold and steaming from anger. Maybe if I couldn't be an Act of God, I could exercise a little Wrath of God. If nothing else, maybe I could put a little Fear of God in someone. At very least, some Fear of Me.

I stowed my bucket and headed to the trailer park. Maybe one of Los Despredatores knew who had had the bad sense and minimal artistic skills to deface my house.

I had a fair idea where they'd be hanging out on a cold Saturday afternoon, but if I hadn't, smell of marijuana and puberty would have led me right to them. I didn't bother knocking but crashed through the trailer's window. It was covered with cardboard, anyway.

I had interrupted their party, if you could call it that. The dingy little manufactured home was littered with bottles, empty chip bags, and drug paraphernalia. Four teens sat in front of the couch, playing Grand Theft Auto, while two couples were on the couch, necking, oblivious to the others. My dramatic entrance sent the girls and one guy bounding over the couch, screaming. Another jerked so hard he unplugged the X-box from the TV. The rest just looked from me to the chaos and started laughing. I didn't blame them; the place reeked of cheap pot.

Dwarvish grunge was playing at full volume. I switched it off. "Where's your leader?" I demanded.

The guy who had jerked out his controller, Mateo, stood up and swore at me in Spanish. "This is my abuela's house!"

"Your grandmother lives in Florida, and your dad can't rent this place because you lot trash it on a regular basis. Don't you ever clean? There's a roach under the couch." One of the girls screeched and jumped onto the chair. "I asked you a question. *¿Dónde está su jefe?*"

Mateo, uncaring about the vermin on the floor, knelt down and tried to plug in his toy. "He ain't here. He's home, singing."

That was not a response I expected. "Singing?"

"Yeah, he's stupid-obsessed with that Mishmash song. So anyway, you got a problem, you can take it up with me."

I had expected more bluster. And more cussing. I'd half-hoped for a fight. But Mateo kept fiddling with the wires. Meanwhile one couple had decided to move to a chair, where they pretended to be paying attention to me, but their hands and unfocused expressions proved they were thinking about other things.

You get what you get, I suppose. Mateo wasn't an idiot most of the time. "Someone defaced my lair. Any idea who it was?"

"Yeah, Rev 13." He snorted, which turned into a girly giggle. He reached for his joint, but he'd spilled his ashtray when I startled him, and it had rolled under the couch. I wondered if roaches got high.

He apparently decided retrieving it was too much effort or too gross to attempt. He settled himself cross-legged and rebooted the X-Box. As it finished its startup routine, he said, "Davey saw them and got some of us, and we chased them off. We spread around that nobody go into your place, too. You gonna thank us?"

"You gonna reform? Do you know who they were? What they looked like?"

"Nah, man. They were all in jackets and hats and stuff."

"Anything? Height? Weight? Age?"

"The jackets weren't that old," one of his co-horts chimed in. The others looked at him like he was an idiot. Then, they all started laughing like idiots.

Fat lot of help that was. Oh, well, at least I could do a good deed or two on my way out. I thanked them for nothing, turned to go, then looked over my shoulder at the couple eagerly awaiting my exit. "Hey. Lisabel, you can do better than that two-timing jerk."

"Two-timing?" she asked, as her date turned red.

I shrugged innocently. "Unless you started wearing Sonja Under Moonlight? I can smell it on his shirt."

As a fight started in Spanish, I turned to hide my grin. If Alberto didn't stop cheating, maybe he'd at least do his laundry more often now. Either would be an improvement. I saw a bag filled with joints and snatched it on the way out.

"Hey!" Mateo protested.

"Aw, do these belong to your grandmother, too? Don't do drugs, kids. And clean up after yourselves." I saluted them and jumped out the window before they could bound after me.

Once I was airborne, I tossed the bag ahead of me and blasted it with a disintegrating-level of fire. It wasn't much, but at least I could say I made a *toke*-en effort.

The next few days, I roamed around Territory, so named by the locals because I'd claimed it as mine, reconnecting with the people and asking about the anti-Faerie riffraff that defaced my home. I didn't get much information. Despite their gratitude to me for cutting down the crime (and the rats) in the area, most were tight-lipped when it came to ratting-out their own kind.

Anna and Frankie Costa, however, kept me well informed about Operation Trap Addison, or Trapison, as they were calling it. I got everything from demonstrations of dance steps to reports of who heard Addison sing what verse. Apparently, she could not contain herself, especially when Anna sang the high note loud and flat.

"So I purposely miss it, as loud as I can. I 'practice' at recess, too. She cringes when she thinks I don't see, but I act all proud. It's making her crazy!"

I warned her against enjoying herself too much, and she called me a spoilsport. One nice side effect, however, was that the kids in her class and Frankie's were more excited about "Bodalicious" than "Mishmash."

Then Greg, Courtney's cousin who was directing the video announced that all the girls should sing the high note and he'd filter out the bad ones. "I can even multiply it, so it sounds like everyone is singing. No one will be able to tell who hits the note and who misses," he assured them.

I wondered if their father's experience in organized crime had rubbed off on them, or if they were just naturally devious. Regardless, if I ever had to frame someone, at least I knew where to go for ideas.

Friday afternoon, I came home from another depressing patrol of removing vandalism to find an email from Greg. The attachment was entitled "The truth shall set us free." That was a good sign. I started to open it, then pulled back. I felt I needed popcorn for this one.

"Bodalicious" was a typical pop song, with a bouncy beat for dancing and lyrics that were tame enough for the kids but adult enough for those who understood the double entendre. You know, stuff like being so fine the boys want to play in your playground, stuff about parties where they "drink my Kool-Aid." Jerry, Senior, always insists that means the singer is a government agent; meanwhile the kids (and I) had to ask what "Kool Aid" was. At any rate, it was easy to see why Addison loved the song so much, and while she pranced around and so convincingly lip-synced, the others sang.

"Lip-synch." I snorted. Even without the mics, it seemed obvious to me she was singing under her breath. But I was a dragon; I could not expect humans to be so observant.

To one side of the video of the kids were graphs showing the live input of the mics, both the lavaliers being used by the kids and the three hanging mics. One mic was hung over the top step where Addison would stand for the finale, the other kids under her pointing up with jazz hands. Its graph marked a low flat plain to the peaks and valleys of the others picking up the majority of the sound.

So it was that when they got to the last famous high note and all the kids went silent except Addison, everyone could see the drop in the mics except the one directly above her. She did hit the note perfectly, though; had to give her that.

When Addison realized what had happened and shut her mouth, the silence was deafening.

Anna broke it. "So you can sing!"

Addison's eyes grew wide, and her mouth worked. For a minute, I thought she'd confess.

Then she said, "I... It's a miracle. 'Bodalicious' is such an awesome song and I wanted to sing it so badly, I broke the spell."

Wow. I should have known. Had to give her points for thinking on her feet. If she ever got past herself, she'd be a force to reckon with.

The kids, however, were not going to let her have an advantage.

"You liar," replied one of the other kids, who Frankie said had been Addison's lackey until the fame got to her head. "I thought I'd heard you singing in practice, and you told me I was imagining things."

"You were! I—" she started, but the others started shouting protests. One child even said he'd thought he'd heard her humming and she'd told him he was crazy like Sister Grace. Either Addison was as careless as she was intimidating, or the Costas had an uncanny ability to pick the right team.

Finally, Courtney, tears in her eyes, shouted. "Stop it! You just didn't like Sister Grace because she didn't make you her favorite. You always could sing. I heard you in the bathroom a day after you said Sister Grace cursed you. And you said if I told anyone, you'd make my life a living, a living, a living HECK!"

And that's when Addison confirmed everything by calling a sobbing Courtney some very filthy words. I did have to give her points for creativity, though it wasn't hard to find a rhyme for "snitch."

Into the shocked silence, Anna said, "Come off it, Addison! You lied and a lot of people are getting hurt. But now we have proof."

Addison looked from them to the mic above her head, then to the camera in Greg's hand. "You tricked me? You said we were doing a nok-nok video! I thought you were my friends. You lied to me. You're all so mean!"

But Frankie was having nothing of it. "You started it. You've been mean to lots of kids. You made Courtney cry all the time. And you lied and lied about Sister Grace. Now people are getting hurt, and you keep lying!"

Addison, however, was crying for the cameras. "I can't believe you'd be so mean. Why do you hate me so much?"

Anna said, "We just want you to tell the truth!"

Addison's former lackey said, "That's not true. You used to be my best friend. But now it's all 'TV this' and 'reporter that' and even if you weren't being so stuck up, my dad won't let me play with you. He works with Faerie people. They're scared, and it's all because of you and your lies."

Addison started to sob louder, but this time, some of those tears seemed genuine.

Frankie added, "You're the one being hateful. We don't want to hate you. We just want you to stop."

Her friend said, "And tell the truth. I know it'll be hard, but if you don't do it now, everybody's going to hate you, forever. Just tell the reporters it was a mistake or a trick, and it got out of hand."

"Yeah!" said Frankie added. "You're a kid. Say the adults got it wrong and you were afraid to say anything. Things will go back to normal in no time."

Addison sniffled, "What about the cameras? It's on noknok now. Everyone knows."

I heard Greg's voice coming from behind the camera. "I'm just recording right now. I won't post it if you come clean. We're not trying to hurt you. We just want the truth to be told. If you want, when all this is done and everyone knows you can sing, we can redo the video."

"Really?" Addison looked his way, eyes glistening. I almost lost my lunch.

"Sure—if you tell the truth. And you promise to be nice to Courtney," he said.

"I'm sorry!" Addison rushed down the step and flung herself into Courtney's arms. The two hugged, sobbing. The boys, looked away, embarrassed, but Anna threw her arms around them both.

That's when the video ended.

I sat back, bemused. That went better than expected.

I should have known better. An hour later, I got a call from a furious Jerry Costa.

"What did you get my children into?"

Chapter Fourteen: Despredators Measures

The Costa house is an eight-bedroom Victorian home in one of the oldest neighborhoods in Los Lagos. In Dona Elena's waning years, it had grown dingy and neglected and full of cats and spite. Jerry and Rita had cleaned it up and filled it with children and laughter.

But there was no laughter today. As I landed on the back porch, I heard kids crying in their rooms—angry and subdued. They must have been crying for a while. That was not a good sign. Neither was the sounds of Rita and Jerry arguing. Maybe this wasn't a "come on in and make yourself at home" situation. I decided to go to the front and ring the doorbell.

A scampering of feet and bedroom doors accompanied the slap-slap-slap of someone stomping in house slippers. Rita flung open the door and greeted me with such rage, I was sure she'd breathe fire if she could.

"You! What have you done?" she shouted.

Behind her, a frazzled Jerry pleaded with her in Spanish for calm. "At least let him in."

She flung her hands in the air and stormed into the hallway. I followed. JJ, Anna, and Frankie peeked out at me from the second floor banister. Their eyes were huge and red-rimmed, but the set of their mouths spoke of suppressed fury that rivaled their mother's. That meant only one thing.

"Addison didn't repent, did she?"

"Repent?" Rita rounded on me with so much aggression, I actually jerked back. She may not have been related to Dona Elena by blood, but the two were cut from the same cloth. Jerry must have had the same taste in women as his uncle.

"Repent?" she repeated, both aghast and accusing. "The only one who should be repenting is you, Vern! Influencing innocent children to perform such a horrible trick!"

"But mama," Anna protested from the safety of the stairs. "We told you. It was our idea."

"Do not interrupt!" Rita said, reaching to pull off her slipper. The kids shrank back. Mama Costa was old school in her enforcement.

Jerry spoke into the momentary silence. "Addison's parents called. She's distraught."

"They want us to apologize!" Frankie cried with righteous indignation. "In front of the whole school. Addison gets away with lying to the whole world, but we catch her, and we get punished?"

"Have they seen the video?" I asked. "She sang. We have proof. She even admitted it."

Jerry said, "Her parents are asserting that it was faked, and Addison was so upset, she was willing to agree to anything to get away from the kids. They're threatening to sue us and the school."

I tried not to roll my eyes. I was sensing a supervillain in my future. Addison certainly was a marvel.

Jerry said, "I know you're new to the Mundane, Vern, but cyberbullying is serious. Kids kill themselves over it."

JJ called from the stairs. "But Papi! It's not like we were making fun of her. We didn't call her anything but a liar and told her to apologize."

Anna added, "It's not even posted. I'm not a cyberbully. I'm not!" and she started crying again.

Rita again shouted at me. "You see? You see the trouble you've caused?"

I wondered briefly if she'd go at me with her slipper. It was plaid and said "BEAR" in bold fuzzy letters. The other said "MAMA." The kids had told me in the past that the bear slipper was the one to watch out for. I held my ground, but I didn't speak, either.

She continued, waving the house shoe like a judge's gavel. She had a lot to say about how I'd broken her trust, letting her kids get involved in cyberbullying, making the family a target of the Lukas' vendetta, and even worse, hiding the whole caper from her and Jerry. She concluded, "You had no right! I know you wanted to help Sister Grace and I supported that, but there had to be other ways!"

As she stopped to breathe, I replied. "You mean like bringing in a qualified mage of the Inquisition to determine the truth of Addison's accusations? Or maybe trying to convince her to come clean on her own? As long as she's getting attention, Addison is going to stick to her story until she gets caught. Even after, apparently. Plus, she was using her newfound fame to make life miserable for the kids. And Anna's right. They're not cyberbullies. They're a group of kids trying to use the power of social media to right a wrong. Did you see the video? They gave her every chance to come clean on her own, and they haven't posted it yet."

"Addison's the bully!" Frankie added. He had an arm around his sniffling sister. "She was always mean to kids she didn't like. She made Courtney cry all the time."

Rita shouted in Spanish for him to be quiet, then returned to me. "It doesn't matter that she lied! They tricked her. They made her think they were her friends."

"I was her friend!" Addison protested.

"We would have been her friends if she would have stopped being a lying liar!" Frankie added.

"*Callate!* Do not pretend you did not lie—and what does the Bible say about lying?" She directed that last to the kids as well as to me. We all shrank back.

"Okay," I said. "So we lied about the video—but what other options were there? Your kids saw a way to fight for justice when the adults couldn't. I advised them. I admit it. But you were the ones who raises strategic thinkers with big hearts."

"And you took advantage of them. They are children, Vern. They don't understand the consequences of what they've done, but you should. Get out. You are not welcome here, anymore."

"What?" The exclamation came from my lips, the kids, even Jerry.

She outshouted us all. "I said, 'Get out!' I don't want you around my children."

She rushed me, brandishing the bear slipper as the children shouted protests. Staying would accomplish nothing. I left.

As I took off, I heard Frankie wailing, "It's not fair! Addison wins again."

He thought he felt bad? I was an immortal drake bested by a narcissistic fourth grader.

As I flew home, I reviewed the situation. I didn't get it. We'd caught Addison in a bald-faced lie, and we were in the wrong for setting it up so she could out herself? I had half a mind to tell Greg to post the video—what's the worst thing that could happen?

I sighed. For all my wisdom, I was a Faerie creature. I still didn't understand all the consequences of the Mundane world—as this evening showed. Maybe I should talk to Father Rich first. I'd probably get another lecture.

And speaking of the homilist, my phone rang with his number.

"Be straight with me: Do you know where Sister Grace is?" He sounded tired.

"I may be able to get a message to her," I hedged.

"Good enough. Santry dropped by the parish. I don't know what's happened, but the Lukases are out for blood. They got the city council to put pressure on him. If Grace sets foot in the Mundane, he'll have to arrest her for real."

"For what crime?" I asked.

"I'm not sure he knows yet, but he thinks they're going to try to make a child endangerment case. He didn't give me a lot of details. He approached me in the confessional."

"And you're telling me this?"

"He's not Catholic—plus, he had to be subtle about it, but it was obvious he wanted me to do something."

Obviously, Santry did not understand how confessionals worked, but who was I to question his choice? I promised to do what I could.

I turned toward the north side of town, where there was a band of pixies I sometimes worked with. They could get a message faster than if I were to personally go to Faerie. It was going to cost me the last of my money and maybe some of my blood. Could the day get worse?

I really had to stop asking that question. Ahead of me was a billboard with the leering faces of Acoustic Blenda.

How's your singing? You could win a front-row seat to the Mishmash concert in Los Lagos, Colorado.

Auditions were at ten tomorrow morning, with the concert in the afternoon.

It's not a problem, I told myself. We never found anything wrong with the song. As near as anyone, Faerie or Mundane, could tell, it really was just a bunch of nonsense sounds. Besides, people have been singing it all over town with no ill effects. What harm could it do to get a couple of people to sing onstage with the band? We'll see. Nothing will happen tomorrow, and we'll all have a good laugh. Grace can come back and take the spell off Addison...

But what about what Grace saw? The tentacles or whatever? Either she was hallucinating or something in that song summoned something.

I showed her that tattoo. Did I plant an idea in an already overstressed, paranoid mind? Did I make her snap?

Did I like that idea that much better than the alternative—that she was right, and there was something sinister happening under my nose? Even if there was, who would believe me? I had no evidence, and if the Mundanes would not listen to a human nun, what chance did I have? It's not like I had the best relationship with the local authorities. Santry'd just as soon stuff me in a cell than believe a cockamamie story I can't support.

Hey, God? Would you help a drake out with some direction? Sun shining on the concert hall, gust of wind to point me the right way?

Nothing. Not even a bird.

It was too depressing alone in the air with all that time to think. I was almost to my stop. I dropped down to the street to walk the rest of the way. My feet would get cold, but maybe the chill and the noise would distract me. I could pick up a couple of gallons of midgrade on the way home to warm myself up.

I started to cross the street.

That's when Vialpando hit me with his police car.

Chapter Fifteen: Amazing Grace

I woke up to the sensation of straw tickling my nose. Then I opened my eyes to see Officer Sterling watching me from the other side of a set of bars. I leapt to my feet with a roar. "It wasn't my fault!"

Tracy jerked back. "We know! We know! Just calm down, Vern. We brought you here to take care of you."

She reached out slowly and pulled open the cell door to show it was not locked.

"You what?" I asked, and then the aches hit. "Ow!"

"Yeah... Sebastian was going about thirty when he smacked you. He's really shook up."

"Poor him." I sat down hard. Oh, my ribs hurt. That's when I realized my abdomen was wrapped in tight bandages. Who had done that? Memories were coming back sluggishly as I got oriented to my current, once-again bruised, state of being.

"Well, he is," Tracy insisted. "I mean, it's bad enough that he hit you. You're tough. You should see the car. But what if it had been a child? The captain's furious. Anyway, our vet looked you over and did what he could for your ribs and scrapes and stuff. He didn't know what would work for a painkiller, though."

"Chevron Premium," I muttered. It was going to be that kind of day.

Tracy laughed. "You must be feeling better. Shall I go get Captain Santry? I think he may actually want to apologize."

I barked a laugh. It hurt. I rose, anyway. "I can go to him." No way did I want to spend any more time in a cage than necessary. Besides, I was healing. I'd be sore for a day or two, but barring any big fights, I'd be fine by Monday.

My shoulder was sore, but I did my best not to limp as I made my way to Santry's office. This was how God was answering my prayers, now? I suppose I wasn't all that surprised. However, I did not expect Santry to rise from his seat to greet me.

"How are you feeling?" he asked.

I was not in the mood for his sudden solicitousness. "Like I got hit by one of your squad cars! What is wrong with that man? I hadn't even seen him this week."

Santry maintained the face of calm, but I could hear his heartbeat and feel the rise in his body temperature. He felt almost as frustrated as I did. "It wasn't intentional. He said he zoned out for a minute and didn't see you."

"Didn't see...me? An 850-pound dragon? *In the crosswalk?* What was he doing—texting his optometrist? Or did he drop his cigarette and set fire to his pants?" Come to think of it, it did seem oddly hazy in the car.

Santry's expression hardened and not just from my quip. "He and his partner were singing that damn song."

I felt my blood run cold. Was Vialpando's car smokey, or were there shadowy figures moving around inside that only a Magical—or a mage— might notice? "Mishmash?"

Suddenly, we heard a thundering of footsteps and Charlie Wilmot dashed into the room. "Begging the Captain's pardon but I— Bloody hell, Vern! You really got hit by a car?"

I sighed. "Yep. One to scratch off my bucket list." While he tried to parse out the idiom, I noticed a package in his hand. Even from where I stood, I could smell the sands of Faerie Egypt. "That for me?"

"Oh, yes! The bishop said it was absolutely urgent. I've been looking for you all morning." He handed me the parcel.

Oh, fewmets. Here was my prayer's answer, and given the timing, I had a bad feeling.

"Santry? Does Vialpando happen to have perfect pitch?"

He gave me a querulous look. "Yeah. He sang with a lot of bands in L.A. Why?"

I set the package on the table with a thunk. I untied the cords and pulled the fleece away from the artifact within. What I saw chiseled into the stone made me forget my former complaints.

It was Blenda-guy's tattoo in all its tentacled glory, ripping the lungs out of some mesmerized human. A couple of symbols were written below—an incomplete inscription. A paper folded inside identified it as a tribal ceremony from before Sumer.

Grace had said Addison had perfect pitch.

"She kept singing it, perfectly, start to finish, over and over. And the more she sang it, the less she seemed aware of what she was doing. She kept singing it, faster and better and, and I saw..."

Vialpando had perfect pitch.

I closed my eyes, forcing the memory of the accident back to my mind. Vialpando, his eyes blank, mouth moving, dark tentacles flowing around him.

"Where's Vialpando now?"

"Sent him home."

"Alone?" I almost squawked the word as the lettering on the tablet shifted in my blurred vision and translated themselves into an alphabet of sounds and music: the song "Mishmash."

...tentacles...wrath...return...

Return!

"What time is it?"

"Almost two. What's going on, Vern?"

The concert was at 2 p.m. in Los Lagos—midnight in Faerie Sumer.

"Where's Father Raul?"

"He's heading home." Santry's tone started to match mine in alarm. "What is going on?"

"Find him—and any other magic users in town. Get them to the Mishmash concert, fast. And get someone over to Vialpando's and don't let him sing that song!"

I dashed out of the precinct and took to the air, my injuries forgotten.

Spotlights shone around the crowded concert hall. People hung out outside the doors. I heard the all-too familiar strains of "Mishmash," second verse. Under that noise, Grace shrieked protests as security tossed her out the back. She glanced up, saw me and shouted, "Vern!"

Great. The one mage who would not work magic. Fine. I wasn't going to question God's ineffable reasoning. At least she believed in the danger. I didn't waste my own time with words; I just folded my wings and dove for the door, knocking security guards down like bowling pins. Grace scrambled after me.

We fought our way backstage, dodging wardrobe technicians, make-up stylists, and crew waiting for the next set.

"What are you doing here?" I asked.

"The man who gave us a ride to the convent makes regular deliveries to the sisters. He told Sister Eloise. I came as fast as I could. Where have you been?"

"Long story," I snapped back as we dashed up a flight of stairs. How far was this stage?

I jinked to the left to avoid running down some skinny stagehand asking for a light and turned my head and spat a short flame at his cigarette before rounding a corner. I probably shouldn't have, since we were in the building, but I love showing that trick off. It's a weakness.

Unfortunately, in the process, I didn't see the security guard leaving the snack room. We collided and both went down in a shower of cake, chips, and coffee. Unlike SkinnyCigs, Snackman had enough weight to stop me cold. My ribs screamed in protest.

"Maybe you should lay off the sweets," I grumbled as I untangled myself. I slipped on some icing and cold latte.

Grace shot past me. "Vern! Quit fooling around!"

Yeah, that's what I was doing. Oh, wait, maybe I had been. Figures she'd be right about that, too. I scrambled after her, ripping off my latte-stained bandages as I ran.

By the time I'd gotten to the backstage area, stage right, the song had done one round and started again. The band was no longer playing, just rocking and stamping. The stage crew, too, joined in the song, which no longer sounded like mishmash to me, but a summoning straight from the depths of Hell. The music, on tape, played on at deafening volume.

I looked out into the mesmerized and chanting crowd. I saw Wolf in the front row, entranced. Beside him stood Addison staring in horror at her bespelled mother.

I yelled, "Wolf, Missus Lukas, snap out of it!" Of course, they didn't respond. I thought I saw tendrils, like mist, escape their mouths and envelope them.

"Addison, run!"

But Addison cried and pleaded as she pulled at her mother's arm.

Grace had tried to muscle the mike away from the lead singer and been slapped to the ground for her efforts. She fell hard, center stage; then cried out and crab-walked as far to stage left as she could, shrieking denials and pleas to God the whole time.

The center stage floor had started to pulsate in red and orange.

We had to stop the music. I searched for the outlet, gave up fast, and threw my weight at the sound equipment. Sparks flew as a few thousand dollars' worth of acoustic hardware shattered. Feedback caused the speakers to squeal, then go silent.

But the song went on.

I ran out on stage and roared, pitting my dragon ferocity against the din of the song. I lost. The hundreds of dead eyes didn't even notice my magnificent display. Sure knew how to hurt a drake.

I whirled toward Grace. She'd backed up against the curtain and had pulled it around herself, looking more like a scared child than the religious who once fought in the Great Wars. "Grace! Make them stop singing!"

"I can't," I barely heard her whimper.

The stage floor began to rip. I leapt toward the band, sweeping them up with outstretched wings and flinging them offstage. I spun around as an impossible fountain of lava and fire erupted from where cement and rats' nests should have been. Something shot out with it, and the floor healed itself with a sucking sound that made my stomach turn.

Then there stood Octothulu, in all his slimy, tentacled, 3-D, Technicolor splendor.

Yet kind of puny. Funny. Didn't expect puny.

Better not to question my good fortune. I pounced.

The chanting rose in volume.

A tentacle, thick and pinkish, slapped me from the air like I was an insect. I fell into the center stage curtains. They tangled around me like a net. I slashed and tore at the heavy fabric to get free.

It could not have taken more than half a minute, but that time, Puny had grown to Colossal and was reaching out to a cowering Grace.

"Run!" I yelled. Then I let loose with about 1500 degrees Kelvin of dragon wrath.

I managed to burn off its slime, though not much more. But I did get its attention.

I had just enough time to beg God for help before it swung at me. Or should I say, "they swung"? Twelve tentacles sprouting from its back, four as legs, and another half-dozen making its squid-like beard. I did not consider this a singular opponent or a fair fight.

And it was getting stronger. The singing was making it stronger.

"Grace!" I yelled as I dodged, wove, slashed, and snapped. "You have to make them stop singing!"

"No, I can't," she sobbed. "I can't force another to my will—"

"You did it with Addison, and she's fine!" Sort of, considering she was in the audience with her possessed mother. "It's okay! Really! Sing!"

"Don't make me, don't make me..."

"There's not a lot of choice!" A face tendril got too close. I snapped out, severed the wriggling thing, and spat it out as a body tentacle smashed across the back of my head. I saw stars. It got the other nine around me and squeezed. I felt already cracked bones snap. Fighting pain, I breathed fire into its face. It flung me away with a roar. I skidded stage left, smacked against some heavy prop, and fought off the gray mist of unconsciousness.

Free of the annoying thing trying to stop him, the monster slithered toward the audience. Their chanting continued, but slower, duller. The audience was tiring, and the spell weakening with them. It wouldn't sustain the monster much longer. It'd find nourishment by other means.

I tried again. "Grace. Do something. Shield the audience. Banish the beast. Something! I know you have magic. Use it!"

"I can't, I don't..."

Nightmare of the Black Lagoon hesitated at the edge, wriggling tentacles exploring the drop. It let out a low, beguiling moan. The crowd surged forward, fell back slightly, then surged again, like waves obeying the pull of the moon.

I tried to rise, felt muscles tear and give out. I tried to breathe fire but spat out blood instead of flame. "Grace! It's going to attack the audience! Do something!"

Her breath came out in gasps so fast she couldn't even talk.

The undulations of the crowd had brought the front row within a few feet of the creature. I heard a familiar voice wailing for her mother to wake up. Addison!

"Grace! Look at the audience. There are children in it!"

"I..." She managed a moan. She stared at the monster with terrified eyes and cowered behind the velvet curtain, a tiny fish hiding from the giant squid. I thought I'd seen a fighter in her. I was wrong.

Snarling a curse at St. George, the bishop, and anyone else who'd led to my being in this mess, I gathered my three good legs under me and propelled myself at the beast. I knocked it back and off its...whatever. I bit and scratched and roared yet barely managed to keep it focused on me. Then it lifted me over its head and flung me onto the stage, my broken wing under me and my belly exposed. It pinned me with its tentacles as the tendrils curled away from the face to reveal a sharp beak.

Dragons don't die, but we can be painfully inconvenienced. And was I going to be painfully inconvenienced!

"Grace!"

The audience had started to crawl onto the stage. Addison's mom was one of the first. Addison followed, trying to push her back down. She was sobbing so hard, she could barely speak. Then Wolf grabbed her by the waist and threw her into Squidthulu's line of sight.

Grace screamed.

The scream resolved itself into a single note: A over high C. Then it moved down but gained in volume. The glass in the stage lights shattered, as did the glass on a fire alarm switch. Wouldn't you know? Demon lava and my pyrotechnics didn't spark a reaction, but she hit a high note and the alarms and sprinklers go off. The water shocked the audience out of their stupor. People screamed and stampeded to the doors.

Grace sprang up from where she was hiding and snagged Addison while the monster twitched, as if disturbed by her singing. How was that for karma? Meanwhile, she pulled Addison to her feet and pointed her toward the exit. This time, Addison ran. And still Grace sang.

The note became a melody, the melody became a song, the song became a prayer, the prayer became spell. Grace stood, trembling. With each step, she shook so hard I was sure she'd stumble. Yet her voice stayed clear and strong and commanding with the authority of God and the power of the Holy Spirit.

The creature dropped me like a 90s boy band, and I skittered away, not able to do much more than attempt to look dignified in the process. The creature turned to confront Grace, but all he could do was writhe and snarl and threaten. Grace's voice wrapped around him like a prison, her beautiful clear notes flowing like vines to envelop him. Sweat broke out on her forehead, tears streamed down her eyes, but her song never faltered. The captive creature made one last, ineffective push, and shouted some words I'd never repeat in any language.

Still Grace sang.

Then, when the holy magic of her song had fully surrounded him, she shouted a command, and the creature disappeared. No pyrotechnics, no explosions. Just a peaceful little *pop!*, like a soap bubble on a summer day.

The audience stopped their wild stampede and turned around in the sudden stillness.

Then they cheered.

"Don't just stand there," I croaked. "Take a bow."

Chapter Sixteen: Saving Grace

I must have blacked out sometime during the ovation because the next thing I knew, Grace was kneeling next to me, sobbing apologies.

I ached everywhere. I was bleeding from multiple wounds. My vision kept darkening as I fought unconsciousness. I was craving calamari. I didn't need her regret. I was regretting enough for the both of us.

"Grace. Healing spell. Sing."

"I... I don't..." Her eyes were wide and confused.

Great. Saving Grace was gone again. At least Squidthulu was banished. Figures. Defeat the monster, and I don't even get to eat him. "Pray."

She set her hands on my flank and whispered urgent prayers.

In the meantime, someone else pushed hard against my shoulder. I turned to snap at them and realized Wolf had pulled off his T-shirt and was pressing it against an open wound in an effort to stop the bleeding. He looked almost as frantic as Grace. "What do I do, Vern? What do I do?"

"Healer," I gasped out. "Food!" With no alternatives, dragons will burn calories and magic to heal. With only a trickle of magic flowing through the Gap, I needed nourishment fast or I might start eating the lookie-loos within chomping distance. There were quite a few of them, now broken free of the Mishmash spell but standing around dumbfounded, nonetheless.

His hands still pressed firmly against my wound, Wolf turned to yell at them. "You! Idiot with the cell phone. Stop filming and call 9-1-1! Everybody else—find food. Burgers, hot dogs. Whatever."

"With whose money?" another idiot asked. He was so close to my teeth. I growled.

Wolf shouted obscenities. "He just saved all our freaking lives! Get him some food!"

Mrs. Lukas showed up with a first aid kit, one of those hand-held boxes. Pitiful against the extent of my injuries, but she fed me every pain killer in the box, ripping apart the little plastic packages as fast as she could. Wolf did an inexpert job of taping his shirt to my shoulder then attacked other wounds. In the meantime, he bullied two guys into pulling down a curtain to lay over me.

Addison sat beside Sister Grace, her arm around the nun, and added her own prayers. Grace was shaking as hard as I was. The guys snagged another heavy curtain to wrap around her and Addison.

Someone ran up with a box of donuts. The security guard I'd crashed into earlier. It hurt to laugh.

I managed to down them all, a bucket of nachos, and a pile of burgers before I heard the sirens and the police came crashing through the door. When seconds count, right? At least they'd found Father Raul.

I had just enough energy to be grateful, then blackness overtook me.

"Vern?" Father's tentative query grated against my ears.

"Food," I responded, eyes screwed shut against the pounding of my skull. Beneath me, I felt a familiar comforter over carpet rather than the cool boards of the stage. I'd been moved to Father's study. I didn't know how long I'd been out, but it wasn't long enough.

"Come on, Vern..."

"Food!"

A tray was shoved under my nose. It smelled delectable. I dug in. Ribs, chicken, brisket... All a little dry, not that I was complaining. I'd take Natura's day-old scraps to stadium burgers and stale donuts any day.

Another scent inspired me to open my eyes. Coffee! Black, strong, and poured into a shallow bowl. Father Rich knew me well.

But I knew him, too. Something was wrong, and he needed me. I lapped up the coffee while I took stock of my injuries. I didn't feel nearly as bad as I expected to. I could breathe easily, and my wings only ached distantly, like the memory of a broken bone. I was taking up my usual amount of the blanket, so I hadn't lost much size. That meant one of three things:

1. Someone had ponied up the money for a first-class healer

2. I'd been out a long time

3. God needed me for something, probably something I would not enjoy.

Resigning myself to the inevitable, I sat up a bit and thanked Father and Sister Bernadette, who was refilling my bowl with a fresh pot of coffee. "How long have I been out?"

"Just a day. I'd have let you sleep longer, but Sister Grace—she's in a bad way. We were hoping maybe you could reach her."

"Where is she?" If she was in jail, I and Santry were going to have a conversation...at 5,000 feet in the air.

But Father said, "After Father Raul did triage on you, they piled you into a van to bring you here. Sister Grace wanted to check the area to make sure there weren't any more signs of the demon, but she was so shaken up, Santry escorted her back to her apartment. Because it's a transition home, reporters have to keep their distance. He thought she'd be where she could get some help dealing with what happened, but... Well, you'll see."

Father offered to drive me, and since I felt weak and a little dizzy, I didn't argue. Of course, as soon as we stepped outside into the glare of camera lights and the cacophony of questions, I regretted not launching off the roof. How many times had I saved lives—saved both the Faerie and Mundane universes, for that matter—yet this is the time they want to make a big deal out of it.

"Vern!" one reporter outshouted the rest. "How do you respond to the accusations that you and Grace McCarthy destroyed the stage at the Acoustic Blenda concert?"

Oh. I should have known. I prayed for patience. These were the times it was not good that I could breathe fire. "It's *Sister* Grace, and if anyone was destroying things, it was the monster tossing me around like a chew toy while I tried to keep it from eating the audience. A monster that Acoustic Blenda and its audience summoned by singing a song *Sister* Grace had been warning people about for weeks."

"There was almost five thousand dollars in damage," someone called out—Kitty McGrue; I recognized her nasaly snark. "Who's going to pay that?"

We saved Los Lagos from a demonic being—and with less damage than the Avengers, I might add—and she was worried about who was paying for the damages. Well, it wasn't going to be me.

"Maybe they can bill Squidthulu? We all know how you can reach him now, don't we?"

Behind me, Father stepped on my tail, the equivalent of a warning kick under the table. I didn't care. My head hurt and Grace needed me. I had better things to do than answer asinine questions from people who hadn't been there.

"Experts are saying it was mass hypnosis—comment?"

Mundanes. I was too angry to even roll my eyes. "Mass hypnosis did not throw me into a pillar. Mass hypnosis did not break my ribs. It was a monster, summoned by a song that was in fact a spell so ancient even I'd forgotten what it was. The sooner you Mundanes understand that magic is real and potentially dangerous, the sooner we prevent this and my vet bills will go down."

That earned a chuckle, but someone else protested, "Then what about the concert in L.A.? Nothing happened there."

"There's no magic in L.A. We're right by the Gap! Magic trickles in. That sparked the spell." I sighed to myself. Someone really needed to write a pamphlet.

The questions came hot and fast, then, as did my snark. How did I explain a spell getting into the hands of a previously unknown band? (How should I know?) Had the families of the victims contacted me? (What? While I was unconscious?) Why did we decide to interfere with the concert after the being was being summoned instead of reaching out beforehand? (Sister Grace had tried for weeks, not that anyone was listening.) If there were any good questions, they were drowned out by the ignorant ones.

I'd had enough. As soon as Father let pressure off my tail, I took to the skies. The press conferentation had given me a headache on top of my dizziness, but no way was I showing weakness as I ascended. I'd hide among the clouds, land in some alley, and throw up privately before heading to Sister Grace.

Later, with a clearer head and a more settled stomach, I made my way to Grace's apartment.

Magic congealed around the building, as if called, and it was...not evil, but broody and protective. I seldom sensed emotions in magic. I had a bad feeling about this.

That feeling was justified when I got closer and saw the two men hanging out by their car near the entrance. They may not have had white medical coats, but something about the way they stood with arms crossed as Indira spoke to them said, "orderlies." A police car was pulling up behind them. Another bad sign.

Too top off everything, my favorite demon was lounging on the edge of the nearby building, legs swinging over the precipice, his gaze flitting impatiently between the orderlies and Grace's room.

Well, I knew how to handle Acediadeus, but I needed a gift. I took a detour. Ten minutes and fifteen dollars later, I landed next to him, a brown bag held in my tail.

"Leave Grace alone," I said without preamble.

He tsked like a snotty preteen. I wondered if he'd been watching Addison. "Who said I was going after the nun?"

I shrugged. "Maybe you aren't. Maybe you're going to possess one of those orderlies down there, and once they get Grace into that car, take over and drive her across the Gap and deliver her to your brethren. What do you think will happen then? Think you'll be hailed as a hero? Forgiven? That's assuming Grace doesn't fight you herself—and she did just banish a monster—and the police escort doesn't stop you, and you can drive that hunk of junk through the TSA barriers on the Gap... Well, now you have me to contend with as well."

Acediadeus glared at me with narrowed eyes, but I knew I was right. We had a long history. In the Great War, we'd fought a battle that left me with 100 years of depression and indigestion and him with the stigma of perpetual failure and banishment to the Mundane. Since my emigration, we've had an uneasy, Casablanca kind of detente: a down-and-out dragon detective trying to do good and a burned-out demon who'd lost his motivation to do evil.

Still, he did have a modicum of pride. "What's in it for me if I don't?"

"I brought you the good stuff." I handed him the bag.

Greedily, he pulled out the bottle it contained, then frowned. "This is the good stuff?"

"As good as I can afford right now. I was going to spend it on a couple of gallons of premium for me, you know."

He read the label. "Fireball whiskey."

"You can have that fireball, or I can treat you to a real one," I offered.

"Ha. Ha. Why do you care, anyway? She's none of your business."

"Well, I'm making her nun of my business now."

He grimaced. Puns. The bee stings to the demon psyche. It's even worse if you pretend they weren't deliberate.

He tried again. "She's more trouble than she's worth."

"For you, certainly."

He glanced from the bottle to me and back to the bottle. I knew I had won. One of the weirder punishments Satan had put upon him was that he was not allowed to get his own liquor, so if he wanted to indulge his gluttony, someone had to give it to him—without coercion. Finally, he said a curse word that didn't make much sense in hell. "My brothers would probably take the credit for catching her anyway. She's all yours—for now."

"You're too kind," I said because I know how it annoys him. He threw me a not-so-kind gesture and disappeared.

Chapter Seventeen: Grace Under Pressure

I glanced in the direction of Grace's third-floor apartment and the magic surrounding it. Repulsion shield, but badly done, like it was forged more from desire than skill. Made sense, considering how out of practice she was. It struck me, though, just how lucky we were against He Whose Tentacles Must Not Be Counted. God intervened, for certain.

No point dwelling on that. Time to deal with the Now. I could almost feel the repulsion shield from my perch, like an itch. No wonder Acediadeus didn't get closer. Her neighbor below was probably okay, but I'll bet the neighbors on either side had walls they dared not approach. It was a good thing she lived on the top floor—anyone above her would have thought the floor was hot lava for real.

No mortal was going through her door. I wasn't sure I could. I grimaced. I did not have a choice, did I?

I heard a shout and looked down to see Indira waving at me. Fewmets. I was hoping to deal with her after I'd had a chance to talk to Grace.

I flew down. One of the orderlies gave a start at my presence, but the other pulled out his phone to snap a pic. Once upon a time, I could have charged him $5 for that. Instead I ignored him and instead greeted Tracy, who had come out of her squad car when I landed.

"How are you feeling?" she asked.

"I'll manage," I said. "What are you doing here?"

She shrugged, not quite apologetic. "It's standard procedure. Besides..." She waved a hand at the building.

Indira took up the story, explaining how Grace had come home, upset, refused a sedative, and locked herself in her room. Since then, things had gone downhill.

"We hear her sometimes, ranting, I'm sorry to say. Prayers mixed with self-talk, mostly, but there are times when it's just nonsense. I wanted to go to her, but..." She paused, flummoxed. "I have a key. I can get in. I just can't make myself approach the door."

"It's not your fault. There's magic gathering. It's trying to protect her, I think," I reassured Indira. "Get as close to her apartment as you can—but they stay down here."

I jerked my nose at the two orderlies.

Indira frowned at me. "Vern, Grace has regressed. We don't have the facilities to help her here."

"They stay here," I repeated. I sat down and curled my tail around my legs—the dragon equivalent of crossing one's arms stubbornly.

"We can trust Vern," Tracy added.

She frowned but gave in. "All right. We'll assess first, if we can."

"Leave that to me." Satisfied, I took off toward her window.

About two feet from the window, I paused to assess the situation. At least that's what I was telling myself. Truth was, I didn't want to get closer. I could feel my muscles tense with the urge to flee—me, an apex predator! This was not a nun to mess with.

But somehow, Sister Grace had gone from none of my business to nun of my business, and there was no escaping now. Besides, she needed me. She was obviously scared, and who better to protect her than an apex predator on the side of God?

Pride didn't stop me from trying the easy way, though. I called out, "Grace? It's Vern. I'm at the window. How about letting me in?"

Silence. Was she finally asleep? Hovering, I listened. Even that was hard to do through the spell, but I caught the sound of ragged breathing. She was not asleep—but she wasn't moving, either.

This was going to hurt. I moved to the window. It was like swimming in the dragon equivalent of hot lava. I braced myself for picking the lock...then smirked as I saw the latch was not engaged. That was typical Faerie—intense protective magic, forget to lock the window. Or was it a Freudian slip? A Freudian permission slip?

Telling myself puns and jokes to stave off the foreboding, I opened the window and slipped in. Have you ever seen in the movies where someone moves through a wall with a device that rearranges their atoms to slide between those of the wall? Only the device doesn't work correctly? Crossing the threshold was a lot like that.

Once I'd pulled my tail through and my head cleared, I glanced around the room, taking in the harp and discarded sheets of music, the over-turned bottles of pills on the table. Not good. I called again. "Grace? It's Vern."

A sharp intake of breath answered me, as if she wanted to call out but was afraid to. Well, at least she knew who was in her apartment. I moved slowly to her bedroom, calling out reas-surances all the while. I found her on the other side of the unmade bed, knees under her chin and her arms wrapped around them, shivering, staring at nothing, trying to make herself small and hidden. She even had the ends of her wimple pulled around her face, as if to protect her mouth.

I settled down in front of her, catlike, so my face was at her level. "Grace?"

She looked up.

"They'll come for me now," she whispered. I thought she meant the orderlies, but she contin-ued. "They know what I did. What I can do.

They'll take me again and try to twist my voice, and I dinnae know if I can..." Her teeth started to chatter, making her unable to finish her sentence. She ducked her head again.

You're not the only one who was hurt in the Great War. Her words made sense now.

I rose and slunk around her, surrounding her protectively with my bulk. "I'm here, now." I told her.

"There's a demon outside. Waiting," she managed to say.

"Acediadeus? Don't worry about him. I chased him off."

Surprise made her stop shivering. "Ye did?"

"It wasn't even that hard."

She peered at me skeptically. "Should I ask?"

"I'll tell you all about it another day. Right now, just know I've got your back," I reassured her.

Her skeptical look remained. She even snorted. "Ye have my back? Seems to me I saved your back against that monstrosity."

That was the Sister Grace I'd come to know. I chuckled. "Even more reason to not be afraid. You are a force not to be reckoned with."

She was still strung tight with anxiety, but at least she was able to talk more easily. "There will be others. They can't afford to let me go. They had plans for me. They said..."

"The war was a long time ago," I spoke soothingly. "More than a century. Even demons move on."

"It does nae feel like that long ago," she replied.

"Yeah, well, that's what happens when you sleep for a hundred years. Besides, we're in the Mundane. They have to play by different rules here."

"Like tricking a band into singing a summoning spell?"

I hummed an assent that was half-purr, then continued to purr. Purring tended to relax most mortal species. "Or using someone's fears and doubts against them."

"Like now?" She started to sniffle.

I replied gently but firmly. "Like now. I'm not sure you realize the strength of the repulsion field you've set up, but you're spooking the neighbors."

"It was keeping the demons out."

"It's also keeping Miz Mason from reaching her remote, and she's already missed *Los Lagos Today* and her favorite game show. That is not a happy woman."

Grace giggled, but they quickly turned to sobs. "I'm scared."

"I'm right here."

I thought she'd throw herself against my shoulder and cry, and had reached out with my tail for the tissue in preparation for the flood of tears and snot. She did lean against me, as if taking strength from my comforting bulk, and took her cross in both hands and started muttering prayers until she could recite them smoothly. Then, she took a final cleansing breath and sat up. She looked around, but I knew she was not examining the room so much as the magic surrounding it.

"Oh, my. I really made a hash job of this, didn't I?"

I shrugged. "You're out of practice, and the magic that makes it into the Mundane isn't quite the same as in Faerie. Trust me, though. It was plenty strong."

She nodded in acknowledgment of my words and the implied compliment, but her mind was already on the spell. She started to hum, and I felt the magic respond. Soon, the spell was under her control and focused on reacting to threats rather than shoving everyone and everything out of the way.

"Better?" she asked.

"Better. And none too soon. There are geese headed this way. You'd have thrown them off their migration route."

She smacked my flank lightly even as she giggled. Then, she leaned back against me, weary. We stayed like that for several minutes, me purring, her breathing easily. It would have been nice, if there weren't a concerned therapist and two orderlies outside, probably checking their watches impatiently. However, since Indira had not knocked, I figured she either had not noticed that the repulsion field had changed or she was afraid to press her luck. Just as I'd decided I should broach the subject, Grace sat up.

"All right, then. What's next?"

"Let Indira in?"

"This will be fun." Grace sighed but stood and went to the door. I followed her out and straightened up her music and the couch pillows while she scooped all the spilled pills into a single bottle and screwed the cap shut. She clutched her cross tightly as she opened the door and poked her head out. "Doctor Prakash? You may come in."

I listened to the clip of the therapist's high heels—steady but hesitant. She was clearly spooked but determined to do her job. This was probably her first time dealing with someone with magical abilities. I wondered if she was going to be up to the challenge. If not, she'd have to reconsider her career choice or her location.

She paused at the door and peeked in. I'm not sure what she was expecting but all she got was me, a remorseful nun, and a semi-neat apartment. Even so, Grace had to repeat her invitation along with a reassurance that it was all right before Indira entered.

Grace went straight to the kitchen and put a kettle on, scooping up her pill bottles and putting them in the cabinet as she took out two cups and a bowl.

The action was not lost on Indira. "Have you been taking your medication?"

"Yes. I took them last night as prescribed and this morning. I also took an extra of the anxiety meds. Doctor Escriva at Walter Reed had told me I could do that on occasion."

"I offered a sedative when you returned from the concert."

Something in the banal way she said that made my hackles rise. "Returned from the concert?" How about "Returned from banishing an ancient evil using magic she'd been avoiding for over a century?" How about "Returned from saving the lives of people who didn't believe her when she tried to warn them?"

Out of the corner of my eye, I saw Grace hesitate, her back to Indira and her fist tense against the box of tea she was grabbing, as if forcing herself not to crush it in her grip. Then, the moment was gone, and she pulled out three teabags. She replied with airy calm, "That's why I took the anxiety pill. A sedative would have clouded my mind, and I needed my wits sharp."

"Why is that?" Indira asked, and in my mind, I heard Admiral Ackbar's voice calling, "It's a trap!"

Grace walked into it. "The spell. I regret that I'm out of practice. It was only meant to repel any demons that might come after me now that I've broadcasted my abilities again."

I had to admit I was impressed at how calm and practical she sounded. Nothing about being afraid to the point of cowering in a corner or about her inability to keep her emotions from impacting the magic she had called to her.

Indira did not reply; hoping, no doubt, that Grace would fill the silence with something more. But she simply occupied herself with making the tea, pouring the boiling water into each cup and my saucer, pulling out the honey, then setting everything on a tray which she brought to the table. She sat down, her expression as pleasant as it was taciturn, and sipped at her tea. It struck me again that she did not trust Indira as a psychologist.

A moment later, I understood why.

Indira toyed with her cup, then set it aside. "Sister Grace, with all due respect to your vocation, you do realize that the real demons are here." She tapped her forehead. "And here" She placed a hand on her heart.

I almost spat out my tea. I'd have laughed, except I could feel the anger rising in Grace. She set her cup down with deliberate slowness and leaned toward her therapist.

"With all due respect to your vocation, doctor, you are wrong. You Mundanes may not see them but trust me; demons are very real."

"There was one hanging out on the roof of the next building over," I added.

Indira turned to me with a patronizing look. "I'm sure your heart is in the right place, Vern, but it does not help to play into Grace's fantasies."

"Fantasy?" Grace shot up from the table with a speed that made Indira flinch. "You think all this was my imagination? I suppose the monster I banished was just a fantasy, too?"

Indira held up her hands placatingly. "Calm down, Grace. Perhaps that was too strong a word. I apologize. You've been through some trauma, and you're struggling to put it in terms..."

Grace laughed. "Trauma. What do you think, Vern? Did a 'trauma' throw you against a wall and crack your ribs?" She turned back to Indira. "Perhaps you'd like to tell me next that dragons don't exist?"

"Monsters are real," I added. "As are demons. As real as I am. As real as magic is. In Faerie, they don't always hide in the shadows or work their evil only inside people's minds and hearts—and thanks to the link between the Faerie and Mundane, you may be seeing more of them."

"Be that as it may," Indira said, acquiescing without admitting we were right, "the important thing right now is how you are, Grace. Your behavior has me concerned."

Grace sat down, regretful and apologetic. "I am sorry about the shield."

Indira reached out and grasped her wrist. "It's not just the shield," she said with gentle earnestness. "Last night you were ranting."

"Ranting? What? No, I—"

"And your behavior over the last few weeks has been erratic," Indira concluded atop of her. "I'm afraid—afraid for you, Grace. Things are not working out like we'd hoped."

I felt a spike of panic rise in Grace.

"What does that mean?" I asked, even though I guessed the answer. After all, the orderlies were still waiting outside.

Indira kept her compassionate gaze on Grace. "I think we should get you somewhere where we can do a more intensive reevaluation—"

"No!" Grace pulled her hand away from Indira. "I am not backsliding, and I am not going back to a mental facility."

"I'm afraid that while you're under my care here, you are under my rules. It really is for the best."

"Yeah, I don't think so." I stood up to draw their attention to me. "Grace, pack your things. Indira, get together whatever paperwork you need for Grace to discharge herself."

"I can't recommend this," Indira said.

"Against medical advice, then. I'll take full responsibility," I told her.

With a shrug, she rose, thanked Grace for the tea, and left.

Grace stood, blinking at the closed door as if she couldn't quite comprehend what had just happened. "So what now? Where do I go?"

"Do you want to go back to the convent in Faerie?" I asked. "I'm sure you'd be welcome."

She hesitated. "I'm not sure it's the wisest choice."

I nodded. I didn't doubt they could protect her against the demons from without, but Indira was right. Grace still had inner demons to contend with. She still needed the help the Mundane had to offer—and she needed a protector. Besides, I could use a good repulsion shield to keep the vandals away. "Then come home with me."

Chapter Eighteen: My Sister's Keeper

"With you?" Grace repeated. "In the warehouse?"

"I know it's not much," I said, "but there is a working bathroom and a camping cot..."

"I'm sure it will be fine," she hastened to reassure me. "At least for me. But, Vern, it's your lair. Your home and your business. Are you sure you'll be okay with the intrusion?"

Was I? I honestly didn't know why I'd volunteered my home. Some instinct told me she needed protecting. Needed me to protect her. But there was something else too. What was it Bishop Aiden had said? That he wanted me to continue to be interested in her? For whatever reason, I was. I'd started to sense a kindred spirit in Sister Grace of Our Lady of Miracles, and despite the many people I'd gotten to know in the Mundane, I didn't think any could "get" me like she could.

Aloud, I said, "We'll try it for a while, until you're feeling more secure."

She nodded, but there were tears in her smile. "All right, then. Sit and finish your tea; this shan't take but a few minutes."

She turned and started pulling out her tea, pills, and other dry goods from the shelves, arranging them on the cloth. In the center, she placed a mug. It had the serenity prayer, but the last line read, "and a strong cup of tea while I contemplate the difference." Finally, she added some dishcloths and an embroidered tablecloth, all of Faerie linen. There was a plastic tub in the bottom of her pantry. Everything fit in it.

By the time she'd finished, her smile had become genuinely happy. She hummed to herself as she pulled the children's drawings from her bulletin board and stored them with her harp music, then unscrewed the legs from the harp and stowed everything in its case.

She headed to the bedroom just as Indira showed up with the paperwork.

Indira looked at the tub and the harp and sighed. "It's against my better judgment to allow this," she told me as she set a stack of papers on the table and took a seat.

"I don't think you get a choice," I said. "Don't worry. She's stronger than you think."

She nodded thoughtfully. We sat a few moments in silence. Then, she turned her head toward the bedroom. "Is she singing?"

I nodded. "She channels magic through her voice. It's how she banished the monster at the concert."

"What is the...magic doing now?"

I could see the effort she was making to believe in something her experience said did not exist. I gave her credit for trying. "Nothing beyond the shield, which is modified by the way. Miz Murphy should be able to watch her shows."

Indira gave me a small smile, but her mind was still on Grace. "She's been here seven months, and I've never heard her sing. Her records said she wouldn't. She never explained why. She never did open up to me. She trusts you."

"We understand each other."

She nodded. "I suppose that's why you're listed as her guardian. Even so, I'm not sure you understand how difficult a task you are taking on."

Guardian, me? I was offering her a place to stay while she figured out her next move. When did I become my Sister's Keeper? I'll bet it was Bishop Aiden's doing, him and his "I want her to keep on interesting you." I was going to have to have a talk with that presumptuous human. Sometimes, he could be just like his brother, the duke.

I kept my expression neutral, however. "We'll figure it out," I promised, wondering myself what I was getting into as she gave me a list of Grace's medications and the name of her psychiatrist, "just in case."

"I won't be able to help after this," she said. "Not that I have been able to help her much as it was."

"Do not underestimate yourself," I told her. "Mundane therapies got her this far, but there are more things in heaven and earth than are dreamed of in your psychaitries. I'm not sure a Mundane can understand what she needs now."

"And are you *sure* you do?"

Did it matter?

I shrugged. "Maybe enough to help her with the next step? At very least, I can chase off any actual demons and monsters. As for the rest—we'll figure it out."

At that moment, Grace exited the bedroom, pulling a suitcase. She gave Indira a bright smile. "Is that the paperwork ye need me to sign, then?"

A few signatures later, and I really was my Sister's keeper.

♫

When we called Fr. Rich to ask for a ride, he told us that the reporters had left the parish grounds. Grace rode with him while I flew on ahead. If a posse of press wanted to ambush us on my porch, I could chase them off before Grace arrived.

Oddly enough, no one was there. Counting my blessings but also not counting on them lasting very long, I called Father to give the All Clear.

The rest of the afternoon was spent settling Grace in. I'd always been the houseguest in the past; I'd never had someone share my home. I didn't realize how much went into the care and feeding of the average human. It didn't help that Sister Bernadette had come along and was overriding every "it's fine" that came from Grace's mouth. The camping cot would be good only until they got something better, she declared, and further insisted that it needed to be in a separate room where Grace could have some privacy. The unused office in the second half-story of the warehouse was summarily cleared out and its contents added to the general detritus that filled my main floor. While she and Bernadette went at the room with brooms and buckets, Father made a trip to the food bank to fill the refrigerator and shelves.

"You never did that for me," I complained as I watched him put milk in the fridge and pasta and canned goods in the cabinets.

"You can catch your food," he countered.

I snorted. "Rats. That's what I'm allowed to catch. Anything else requires a hunting license I'm not allowed to apply for since I'm not human."

"That reminds me," he said as he folded the paper bag and stuck it under the sink.

"That I'm not human?"

"No, smart aleck. We have a new parishioner—a state trooper. He was telling me about a deer he had to dispose of after it got hit by a car. It made me wonder if we couldn't broker some kind of deal where you can get the roadkill."

"I'm a dragon, not a vulture," I said, but it was a token protest. Who was I to turn down venison, no matter how it became available? "Still, the idea has merit. I can do a service and get a meal out of it."

"Exactly. I'll talk to Paul after Mass on Sunday. Speaking of... Bernie!" he called, "I've got to get going."

Once they'd left, Grace and I shared a box of microwavable mac-n-cheese, along with a rotisserie chicken Father had also picked up for us on his errand run. Afterwards, she cleaned the dishes. When the last fork was in the drainer to dry, she turned to me.

"Vern. You didn't have to do this. You've been so good to me, and now..." She paused and took a deep breath. "How do I thank you?"

After my battle with St. George, in which I'd lost nearly everything that made me a dragon, he'd told me I could only earn my greatness back by good deeds and service to the Church. I had to admit, I'd been wondering what sheltering a nun in need would get me. But I didn't feel like explaining that. Besides, I had something else in mind.

"How about putting a protection spell around this place?"

She smiled. "Maybe even a repulsion spell that works on command? It would come in handy with the press. I wonder why none have come by."

We parted ways; her, to work on the spell, and me, to track down that particular mystery. My part didn't take very long. All I had to do was pull up the local news site and read the top story: *Local Child Recants Accusations*.

Addison and her mother were on Los Lagos Today the next day. We watched on the computer, both dismayed and grudgingly impressed at Addison's latest performance.

"You know, I'm not sure if I should be relieved or annoyed," I said as Sarah Chiu, the hostess, hugged Addison and assured her she was a sweet girl. "All my heroics, and I've been upstaged by a ten-year-old girl."

"At least you're still a dragon," Grace countered. "When everyone thought I was in the wrong, I was 'that nun.' Now that I've saved a life, I'm a mage."

"Welcome to the world of Mundane bias," I said as Mrs. Lukas announced that they'd decided it was best for their family to move.

"Los Angeles, New York, Vancouver," I predicted.

Grace gave me a quizzical look.

"Gotta go where Addison can launch her acting career," I explained.

And sure enough! Los Angeles, it was.

I snickered. "What do you want to bet they'll be too busy to give you a personal apology?"

Grace sighed, "As long as Addison sees Father Rich and makes a good Confession. If she's going to be exposed to a den of vipers, at least she can go in with a clean soul."

I smiled, "Sister Grace-ousness to the end."

She rolled her eyes. "Well, I think we're coming to the end of my graciousness—or at least my patience. Might we turn this off now? I really should be thinking about where I'm going from here."

I obliged, but said, "Public opinion is still divided on whether we're heroes or frauds. We should probably lay low until they realize the truth or the next disaster happens and they forget about us. You have a roof over your head—such as it is—and enough food for a week. There's no rush. Why don't you take a little time off? To process, as Doctor Prakash would probably say."

"Are you sure?" When I nodded, her expression turned from pensive to thoughtful. She drummed her nails on the desk, considering. "All right, then. If you don't mind. But I don't want to overstay my welcome."

"Stay for a novena, then," I suggested. "At the end of the ninth day, if your next move hasn't presented itself, we can reevaluate."

Together, we prayed the novena to Our Lady of Good Counsel, finishing off with the Divine Mercy chaplet. Cheered, Grace decided to brush up on her mage skills by practicing a few simple spells, while I checked up on some leads for cases.

We quickly fell into a routine of prayers and shared meals, then her going off to practice while I worked. She tackled the cleaning and even got me to go through some of the boxes of dreck that came with the warehouse and which I'd been studiously ignoring. Grace sang.

One afternoon, I returned after a brief patrol to find the windows cracked open. The stench when I walked in explained why, but only opened up more questions.

Grace, however, was whistling and content. She presented me with three small bottles. The lids were screwed tight, but that did not completely stop the smell.

I squinted at them. I could just make out the color of magical energies mixed in with the brown and puce. "And these are...?"

"Healing potions," she said proudly, then added with a more self-depreciating tone. "At least, as best as I could make with the items at hand. I'm also a little out of practice."

A little? I swirled the bottle. The liquid inside did not swirl in return. "What's in it?"

"Best ye not ask. I had to get creative, I'm sorry to say."

"Sorry, why? Won't they work?"

"Oh, they'll work," she said with confidence. "It just won't be a pleasant experience. Still, I thought they might come in handy in a pinch."

I picked up the largest jar. It felt too heavy to contain just liquid.

"Maybe we should send one to Vialpando," I said, and she laughed and called me a naughty dragon.

I was beginning to think Indira had her all wrong, and Grace had gotten past the trauma that had haunted her all these years.

Then one night I was awakened by a scream and the toppling of the camping cot.

I scrambled up the stairs and dashed into her room. "Grace!"

She was cowering in a corner, a blanket wrapped tight around her, shivering and rocking. There was no one and no threat in the room.

"Grace?" I approached her slowly.

She shook her head in fast, jerky movements. I didn't know if she was rejecting me or some vision in her mind. I decided to assume the latter.

"Was it a dream?" When she didn't answer, I wrapped myself around her, worming my way between her and the wall so that she was protected by my bulk rather than flimsy paneling. "It's ok now. Tell me. Was it a memory?"

Her breathing was shaky and her words halting, but she spoke. "I couldn't move," she said. "They were all around me. They forced me to look into their eyes and there was nothing in them."

I remembered that trick. More than one demon had tried it on me until I mocked them. The Stare of Existential Ennui, I'd called it, but I didn't think Grace was ready for the joke. "They're not here now. You're safe."

She nodded, but her mind was still in the past. "They tried to take my voice," she whispered. "They got into my head, Vern. And they touched my—" Her hand moved reflexively to her throat. "It burned like acid, but it wasn't real. I fought. I did, and they used it against me. They sang, and it was so empty I longed to fill it. But that's what they wanted. They twisted my voice. And I was alone, I was so alone." Her voice faded and her eyes returned to staring at some horrible memory that had hold of her stronger than that tentacled creature ever had on me.

I wound myself around her more tightly and opened a wing protectively over her. "You're not alone. Not anymore."

I spoke reassurances until she relaxed. When she seemed to be more with me than her terror, I asked, "Who was it?"

She shrugged. "Tragoudious. There were other demons, but mostly him. The others were there to make sure I didn't escape."

"Or turn the tables on them, I'll bet," I said. "How many?"

"Six at first. I lost track after a time. They took turns."

I made an indignant sound. "When I got captured, they only sent four to guard me!"

A ghost of a smile graced her lips. "And did ye escape?"

I shrugged. "Point taken, but still. You're not to be taken lightly."

"I came into my power too soon, you know," she said, and her eyes swam with unshed tears. "A willful child with siren blood is a dangerous thing. The Sisters had to hobble my voice until I had moral training as well as magical. It took years before I had full control of myself and my talent.

"Tragoudious... He stripped all of it away, Vern. He tried to make me back into that selfish little child."

"They failed," I reassured her. Yet, in a way, they hadn't. They may not have converted her to evil, but they had left her broken. But she knew that better than I. "Even when you would not sing, you've always been on God's side. If Tragoudious couldn't convert you in Faerie, during the war, with all the power of Hell behind him, there's no way they can do it now."

She murmured agreement, but her focus turned inward to some dark memory of the past.

She'd done enough of that. I snickered. "I wonder how Trag got punished? What do you think? Forced to listen to a children's choir rendition of 'This Little Light of Mine' on a loop?"

She elbowed my side. "Bad dragon! It's wrong to be relishing thoughts of revenge—even against Satan's minions. Besides, you might give him ideas."

We both fell to giggles. Maybe it was wrong of me, but I hoped Tragoudious heard us.

Chapter Nineteen: Good Graces

I awoke later that morning to another cry from Grace, but this one was more in disbelief and frustration than fear. I ambled into the kitchen where she was drinking tea and reading the paper. "Yes?"

"I didn't know prescience was one of a dragon's talents," she said as she passed me the paper.

It was open to the entertainment section, where a headline declared that Addison had signed on with a big-name Hollywood agent. I snorted. Momma hadn't wasted any time, it seemed.

Addison's father wanted her to finish the school year at Los Lagos, the article said. I thought that was a gutsy position to take. Maybe he wasn't as thrilled with his daughter's potential new career as Momma was? Regardless, the agent was quoted reassuring everyone that they would get to enjoy Addison's "many remarkable talents" on her new noknok channel. Friday at 7 p.m., they'd launch her career with a cover of her favorite song, "Bodalicious," which she'd perform accompanied by several teen and pre-teen stars she'd be working with in the Spring.

"It's so good to make some real friends at last," Addison was quoted as saying.

"Ouch," I said as I read that aloud.

Grace grunted agreement. "That poor little Sarah Jacobson has followed her around, hanging in her shadow, since second grade, I was told. It's a terrible thing for Addison to say, and even worse to have it printed in the paper."

"Maybe she won't find out. Not a lot of people read the newspaper these days," I said as I read further. There was a link to a PleasFundMe account where people could donate to helping her family make the move. I wondered how much of that would go to a new wardrobe and hair products. "One thing's for certain. A lot of people will be watching her noknok video."

And, for the sake of the Costa kids, I would, too. I did not have a good feeling about her personal rendition of "Bodalicious."

I hoped my suspicions would be proven wrong, for the sake of Addison's classmates more than her.

♫

The storyline was nothing like the song, but about a poor little fourth-grader (Addison) who was bullied by teachers and classmates alike until her new "true" friends appeared to take her out of the school and to her personal playground. The style was animated, which I was sure they'd say was due to her inability to get to a studio or maybe as a nod to the 80s, but I couldn't help but notice how it allowed the characters to look almost like her real classmates but with enough modifications to say it was coincidence.

"I don't look like that!" Grace protested loudly as the scary-faced nun in a black habit towered over the terrified Addison, brandishing a ruler that turned into a wand.

"And that's why they'll get away with it," I replied.

The comments were scrolling almost too fast to track them all, but among the usual dribble were a few on the slanderous nature of the video offset by others declaring it a "brilliant social commentary." Naturally, there were a lot of anti-Catholic statements, too.

I was willing to bet that the only thing Addison, her mom, or her agent looked at were the growing number of noks and followers on the bottom of the screen.

It was a long three minutes.

The ending credits claimed the script was created by Addison and Allison Lukas. What a lovely mother-daughter project. Grace threw up her hands. "Does her mother not realize the danger she's putting that child in, indulging her like that? I'll be in my room, praying for her soul and for those poor children she defamed. Unless you want to join me?"

I shook my head. I could see from the pained look on her face that she wasn't just thinking about Addison's childhood. I'd probably be protecting her from another nightmare tonight. But at the moment, I'd gotten an idea.

While she retreated to prayer and wrestling with her own doubts, I sent a message to Bishop Aiden. There was someone I wanted Grace to meet.

I went out for my evening patrol and found an unpleasant surprise waiting for me at my first checkpoint.

"McGrue! Why are you hiding behind a dumpster?" I demanded.

Kitty McGrue, investigative reporter for the *Los Lagos Gazette,* stepped out into the dim light. She had a heavy parka closed tight around her face so only her eyes showed through. Her gloved hands were tucked under her armpits. She was shivering, nonetheless. "Waiting for you. What else?" she snarked through chattering teeth.

I groaned. I was not predictable in my routes. How long had she been waiting? "You're going to catch your death of cold," I scolded like someone's grandmother. "If some hoodlum doesn't kill you first."

Cold as she was, she was not too chilled for a hot comeback. "I thought you kept this area safe. Isn't that why they call it 'Territory'?" She pointed with her elbow at the claw marks I'd scratched on the wall to mark it as my turf.

"I have a better record than the police, but even I can't be everywhere at once. What are you doing here?"

"What do you think? I can't get within a hundred feet of your door. None of us can."

By "us," I gathered she meant reporters. I sighed contentedly. "Yeah. It's been so peaceful at home."

She took a breath to reply, but it came out as a cough. It came out as little puffs of steam.

I huffed a sigh. "Come on. You can buy me a coffee."

"You're all heart."

"Ain't I though?"

There was a coffee shop two blocks away, but the gas station was right across the street. The attendant behind the counter greeted me and when he saw the stray I picked up, told us both to help ourselves to something warm. Soon, Kitty was seated in a cheap plastic chair, her gloves off and hands wrapped around a paper cup of steaming hot chocolate. I sat across from her with a large black coffee that was rapidly cooling.

It took a few minutes for her body to warm up enough that she could talk without chattering. It didn't take the edge off her questions, though. "Why is that nun living with you now?"

"You mean 'the mage'?" When she didn't get my joke, I answered more seriously. "Sister Grace is staying with me until she decides what to do next."

"She didn't flee before they could convict her?"

"Why would 'they' do that?"

She scowled. She hated it when I avoided answering her questions, but apparently, she was too cold to call me on it. Instead, she replied, "My sources say she had a breakdown after the incident at the concert. The doctor called for a car and some orderlies to take her to the state mental health institution."

I shrugged. "I don't know what to tell you about your source. Doctor Prakash released her because the magic was disturbing the patients, and I agreed she could stay with me for a while."

"Is there any way I can ask her myself? Sister Grace, not Prakash. She just claims patient confidentiality."

I liked Indira. She might not be cut out for a world with magic, but she was a good person. "I think that's up to Grace. I can ask her, but I've already suggested she wait until the hullabaloo calms down before giving any interviews."

"'Hullabaloo,' really?"

"I like the word. Very dragony. Of course, to say it in my language, I'd need more room, and I'd probably set the candy aisle on fire." Dragon language often involved the use of flame, just one more reason I was glad I could breathe fire again.

"Hullabaloo," she repeated slowly, as if trying to imagine it in draconian. Finally, she gave up and got back to the topic at hand. "You mean about the noknok video? I know Lukas is saying it's allegory, but it was pretty damning."

I paused to regard her. I didn't like McGrue. She tended to twist my words and show my actions into the worst possible light. Her articles this past week never once credited my efforts in fighting the monster, but were only too glad to point out the damage "I" caused when the beast tossed me around like a play toy. Still, she was good at the investigative side of her job, especially when it did not involve me.

I leaned forward conspiratorially. "Can I tell you something as an anonymous source?"

She almost choked on her hot chocolate. "You're kidding me, right?"

When I didn't rise to the bait, she pushed her cup aside and rested her elbows on the Formica tabletop. "Okay. Shoot."

"Those 'bullies' in the video? Just kids who were trying to get her to tell the truth from the start. If you want a bully, you should ask them who it is. Though I know some won't say anything. They don't want to stir up more trouble, and Addison will be in California soon enough."

"If they don't talk, where's the story?"

"Maybe there doesn't need to be a story. Maybe it's just information to inform your other stories."

She sat back, considering. "I'll keep it in mind—if you promise to tell Sister Grace that I'd like an exclusive."

"I'll pass the message, but I can't guarantee anything. I think Grace does not want to stir up any more trouble, either."

McGrue snorted. "Sometimes the truth itself stirs up trouble. That's the only way to sift through the lies."

True to my word, I passed on McGrue's request to Sister Grace. As I expected, she decided she wanted to wait a little longer before talking to the press. There was one public appearance we could not avoid, however: Mass.

There was a parishioner in my neighborhood who sometimes gave me a ride when the weather was bad, so I called her to see if she'd get us both.

"How are you feeling?" Gianna asked as she opened the back doors to let me in her van. She'd laid out some blankets on the metal floor. She always was thoughtful that way. "I heard you took a real beating."

"It was not one of my finer moments," I admitted. "It was a good thing I had magical backup this time. Gianna, meet Sister Grace McCarthy."

"So you're the mage that banished the demon," Gianna said and took Grace's hand. "I didn't know nuns could do magic."

"Only the special ones," I said.

"That is so awesome. Brr! This wind bites. Hop in and let's get going."

Once Grace was in the passenger seat and Gianna behind the wheel, she took up the conversation again. "So you banished the demon with a song?"

"Monster, not demon," Grace said. "There is a difference, but yes. I did banish it." She seemed at once embarrassed and pleased that someone saw us as heroes.

"Cool. That would be such a handy power. I could think of some people that need a good banishing." She caught the horrified expression on Grace's face and quickly amended. "Just a joke, Sister! Promise. Besides, if anyone bothers me, I can threaten them with Vern."

"What?" I teased from the back, "'I've got a dragon and I'm not afraid to use him'? I'm not sure I get enough free rides for that."

"But it'd be a free meal!" she countered, and we laughed. After a moment, Grace joined in, shaking her head at us like we were wayward children.

And on the topic of children, the Costa kids were all present, sitting in a front pew between their parents as usual. They waved in my direction. I waved back but didn't sit with them. Instead, I took a seat on the other side of the aisle beside Grace. We attracted some odd looks, but I was glad to hear her singing albeit quietly, as if afraid to let herself be heard. One step at a time, I suppose.

After Mass, I insisted on coffee and donuts. I had to get my sugar fix somehow. I settled at my usual spot by the stage, Grace sitting on the steps beside me.

Maria broke away from her siblings and ran to me. "Vern!" She attached herself to my leg like a toddler-sized leech.

JJ started after her, but his mother stopped him and approached me herself. I froze, unsure whose wrath I'd rather face: the mother by letting the toddler hug me or the toddler by trying to extract her. I settled for raising my leg toward Mama. It was an invitation to remove the child herself and made Maria giggle as she was lifted from the ground.

Rita waved a hand at me to say it was all right. "How are you, Vern? We heard about the fight."

I gave her the same response I'd given Gianna, but Rita simply nodded to Grace before turning her attention back to me.

"We were worried, you know? All of us. I... I may have been too hasty when I sent you from our home. I know you are a good dragon. Your heart is in the right place, even if you head isn't always."

"Um, thanks?"

"The children miss you. Jerry and I, too. Perhaps we can move on from this? But no more shenanigans without consulting Jerry and me first!"

Did that include using them as little informers? I shrugged. When would that happen again? "I promise."

"All right then."

And the children, who had all been listening without looking like they were listening, let out a collective cry of joy and ran to us, embracing their mother and thanking her profusely, then glomming themselves all over me. I pretended to tolerate it with ill grace, but truth was, I'd missed the little rug rats.

Then Frankie said my favorite words, "Mami, can Vern come over for lunch?"

"If he'd like. It's Salisbury steak, but we have plenty."

"It was on sale," Anna added.

"Well, in that case..." I started and Rita laughed. "Can Sister Grace come, too?"

Grace held up her hands. "I don't want to intrude."

But Rita immediately assured her she was welcome. "After all, you saved all those people—and Addison and that mother of hers." I could see she wanted to say something more, probably in Spanish and probably using words she did not want her children to spell. But we were in the church, or at least the church dining hall, so she reined in her temper and told the kids she'd be heading home in 15 minutes. They could walk across the street with her or with us.

It warmed my heart when they all elected to accompany us.

Chapter Twenty: For the Grace of God

Monday morning was blustery and cold with a chilling rain that didn't have the decency to turn into snow. Grace and I prayed her novena under blankets on the pile of pillows and mattresses that comprised my bed because it was warmer than the bare cement floor. If it were just me, I'd have been tempted to hibernate. Rita had made sure I was stuffed with Salisbury steaks, and I could have afforded a long winter's nap more than a large winter's heating bill. But I had a human to think about, so after our prayers, we went to the front area, where I jacked up the heat, trusting that God would provide.

The first knock on our door was not a case, however, but the priest I'd sent for.

Father Coco was young and blond, with startlingly blue eyes and slight features that would have made him the perfect choice for a live-action anime. When he spoke, it was with a pleasant French accent. "Vern?"

I hustled him in before he could say anything else. It wasn't much warmer in my home, but at least when he spoke, tufts of steam did not escape from his mouth.

"I was so pleased to hear from Bishop Aiden," he started, then his gaze darted to Sister Grace as she poked her head out of the kitchen. "Ah! Sister Grace! *Enchante.* I'm Father Coco."

He went to her and took her hand, kissing it in the genteel way that was still the norm in Faerie France. Grace looked from him to me and back to him, confused. "Are you a therapist?" she asked.

His smile was warm and loving. "Not as the Mundanes would consider it, but I have certain talents Vern thought might help with your healing. May we talk?"

"Of course. Would you like some tea?"

I expected that they'd want some privacy and was about to excuse myself, but Grace pulled down a saucer along with two tea cups, and I took the hint. I closed the door to conserve the heat. By the time Grace has served us the tea and some donuts we'd brought home from the parish's leftovers, the room had warmed up to reasonable if not cozy levels.

Father complimented the tea, then got down to business. "I know some of what has happened to you. You are a woman of great courage and strength of faith."

Grace looked at her tea, embarrassed.

Father continued, "But it's not always enough, is it?"

She took a deep breath and let it out slowly before answering. "No."

"There's no shame in that. You were under physical and spiritual attack that, that chills my blood to think about. It is a testimony to your trust in God that you are here now."

"And to the care of my Sisters," Grace added. "Plus the 'miracle' of Mundane medicine." She tilted her head to the army of pills lined up on the counter.

He did not contradict her. "Have you taken those yet?"

"No. I was about to when you came."

"Excellent. This will go better if there is nothing to interfere with the spell. Sister, have you heard of the Eye of the Resurrection?"

Grace paused, searching her mind. "It sounds familiar, but..."

"It's a rare Talent; only a few people in a generation may have it, and it's not always recognized and developed. I'm so sorry that there were none of us around when you were first rescued from Hell.

"You probably know this already, Grace, but one of Satan's best and most subtle weapons is to twist our perceptions of ourselves. They make an innocent action appear evil, shroud the most caring impulse with an aura of selfishness. It can cloud us with doubt, hesitation, fear. Even self-hate."

"You think that's what happened to me?" Grace asked. She swirled her tea in her cup and didn't look at either of us.

"You were their direct prisoner for weeks, Grace. How could it not? But my Talent, my charism, is to enable others to see themselves as God sees them—the good, as well as the bad. The beauty and the stain of sin. It's a moment of complete and utter clarity before our Creator."

Grace didn't seem to react, but I could hear her heart hammer in her chest, and I could smell her anxiety.

Father Coco must have sensed it, too. "Grace, Confession cleans our souls, but it doesn't always clear our self-perceptions. You've seen yourself through a glass darkly for too long. Let me share my gift with you. See yourself as God sees you."

She glanced at me.

"I'll be right here," I promised.

She set her cup aside with a decisive motion and set her hands on the table. "What do I do?"

He smiled at her with joy I felt came from the Divine. "Just relax. Give yourself in complete trust to the Lord."

He set his hands over hers. "See yourself through the eyes of the Lord. See yourself as God sees you."

I watched Grace's face intently. Her expression went from neutral to studious. Then her mouth trembled into a smile. After a few blissful moments, she pressed her lips together and tears fell from her eyes.

Father spoke: "You were not a willful child. You were a child, four years old, missing her daddy after a long absence. You never knew why you were not allowed in the ocean. Your nanny was never told. When you swam out into the sea to greet your da, it was indeed the song of a siren that sent those people to fight each other for you, but you were just a child, overwhelmed by an instinct you didn't understand."

Grace let out a sob that was half-laughter.

"See yourself, Grace. See yourself as God sees you: your courage, your brilliance, your love."

It took Grace a few minutes to regain her composure. Father Coco rose from the table, patted her shoulder, then busied himself with the tea. He practically glowed, and the expression on his face was beatific. I hoped someday to see such a look of peace on Grace.

"Thank you," she whispered as he refilled her cup. She took a sip, then spoke again more loudly. "Thank you. Both of you. That was...a gift beyond words. I think I'll need some time to process it all."

I wasn't sure Father Coco understood the Mundane meaning of "process," but he said, "It's my custom after such an experience to spend time in Adoration. I thought I'd visit the local parish. Would you like to join me?"

She smiled at the idea, then turned to look at me, questioningly.

I jerked my head toward the door. Through the window, I saw the snow falling at last. "You two go."

I had been at Grace's side for over a week now. I felt like she was ready to go on her own. Adoration was about as natural a first step as a nun could take. Of course, now the question was, where did she want to go next?

An hour and a half later, I was wishing I'd gone with Grace and Father Coco to the parish. Instead, I was listening to my most asinine case yet and wondering if I would get paid or sued.

I'd answered the door to a woman who greeted with me with hands over her heart, as if silently imploring my help.

"Oh, good!" she said when I answered. "I'm in the right place. Please. I'm desperate. I don't know who else to turn to, and well, when I heard on the news what you and that mage had done, I knew you'd be able to help me. You're probably the only people who could understand my problem."

"'That mage' is Sister Grace McCarthy, a Faerie nun, and she's not here right now. But come on in and tell me your problem." I stepped back to admit her, feeling hopeful. Had our fight against the forces of tentacled terrorism actually helped promote my business? If so, I could almost forgive Acoustic Blenda.

But when I let her into my office, she plopped $200 on the desk, pulled out a frog from her bra, and demanded to know how to turn it into a prince.

I wanted to laugh, but those Franklins would get me a couple of weeks' worth of electricity – and some rat traps. I'd started hearing shuffling among the boxes a couple of nights ago. Usually, I waited until they'd multiplied enough that I could make a meal, but now I had a human to think about. So I stayed as serious as my potential client and her amphibian paramour were and asked her to start at the beginning. By the time Grace returned smiling and at peace, my potential client was alternating between tears and angry rebuttals, I was frustrated, and the frog was strangely still and attentive to her.

Grace took in the chaotic scene and started to back out. "I'm sorry. I didn't mean to intrude."

"Not at all," I insisted, relieved to have an ally at last. I fought very hard to sound professional and diplomatic. I probably sounded like a harried customer service agent. "In fact, Patsy was hoping for your expert opinion as well. It seems that this August, she was in Faerie and had a most interesting encounter."

Patsy, who was caressing the frog and kissing his back, took up the tale of how she was approached while exploring Peebles-on-Tweed (the shopping district) and was asked to rescue a prince who had been bespelled by an evil enchantress and turned into a frog when she stole his kingdom.

"He sounded so sincere—Herald Helmuth, I mean. Obviously, the prince, with his condition... Anyway, he showed me papers, deeds, you know? And maps, letters from peasant children. They seemed authentic."

"I see," Grace said slowly. She did not react with mirth the way I had been tempted to. But then again, I expected her to have more sympathy for someone's troubles, even if they brought it upon themselves by being so gullible.

"I gave Helmuth two thousand dollars. To hire mercenaries. He said I needed to take the prince home and love him through the waxing and waning of the moon, but it's been longer already, and Helmuth never contacted me back and the prince is still... Well, look at him! I'm so afraid something awful's happened, and that, despite all my care...

"Your partner thinks it's just a frog," Patsy concluded. "And I keep telling him that's because the magic is so strong. I mean... Freidrich does not act like a frog. Okay, so he eats flies, but he doesn't try to escape, even when I take him outside. He knows my moods. I don't understand. For the past two and a half months, I've given Prince Freidrich all the love I could. There must be something to this spell I'm missing."

"May I?" Grace asked and held out her hand.

Patsy kissed the frog on the head and offered it reassurances as she settled it onto Grace's waiting palm. Grace gently closed her other hand over top of it. Again, the frog hardly moved. I'd have thought it was sick, but it looked hale enough. Patsy had given me chapter and verse on how well she'd cared for it, following all of Herald Helmuth's advice plus everything she'd learned from internet videos.

Grace moved away, putting a little distance between her and us. She looked the frog over carefully, hovering her hand over it the way I'd seen Mother Superior move her hands over Grace when examining the magical energies around her. Next, she hummed, her fingers moving above Freidrich as if plucking harp strings. We sat quietly, Patsy looking longingly at her frog and me giving longing glances at the money still waiting on my desk.

Finally, Grace sighed. "Patsy, I'm sorry. So very sorry. Freidrich is not a prince. In fact, Freidrich was never human."

"But... the spell!" Patsy insisted. "Helmuth said he was under an enchantment. Besides, he's been my constant companion. He responds to me. I know it!"

Grace replied kindly, "There is a spell. You're right about that. And Freidrich is responding to you. But the spell did not transform him from a prince to a frog. It's a bonding spell. Did they ask you to touch Freidrich in a particular way or say a specific set of words?"

Patsy's anger was dissolving into doubt. "They said it was the standard greeting for a prince of the Black Forest, and then I brought my fingers to his lips." She raised her hand to demonstrate. "I thought he wanted to kiss my hand, being a prince and all."

Grace nodded. "That's probably how they sealed Freidrich to you. That's why he's so passive and attentive. But nonetheless, he is still a frog."

"Well that stinks!" Patsy suddenly went from distraught damsel to outraged customer. "What am I supposed to tell his followers?"

"His what?" I asked. "Patsy, there's no kingdom."

"Yeah, I got that. I mean his online followers. I've been chronicling his adventures and our quest for True Love. I have taken this frog everywhere. I have dressed him up, recorded every cute thing he's done... He has eighty thousand followers! How am I supposed to tell them he'll never be the prince they've expected?"

Grace and I traded looks, both at a loss for words. Freidrich, however, sensed his mistress' distress and leaped from Grace's hands to land on Patsy's arm. Despite her ire, she rubbed his shoulder with a knuckle.

"You know," I ventured, "if he's got eighty thousand followers, then they are probably just as amused by his frog antics as they are his potential for royalty. Plus, when you explain how you were scammed, you'll get even more sympathy votes."

"I suppose," Patsy said, miserable. "I was just, you know, hoping for a prince."

Grace set a hand on her shoulder. "You may not have found a prince, but you do have a faithful friend. That bonding spell is permanent. Freidrich will always be loyal and attentive to you. Whereas real princes tend to be somewhat less faithful."

"And generally broke," I added, "especially if they'd had their kingdom taken away from them by an evil queen."

"Yeah. I suppose I don't need that kind of trouble."

I grunted in agreement. "The people who do need the trouble are the ones who sold you a cut-rate prince. I may not be able to bring you your Prince Charming, but I may be able to bring them to justice."

I got a fuller description of the men and where the transaction took place. I was betting they were long gone—the Frog Prince seemed too complex a scam to play very often. Plus, after two months, the trail would be cold. However, Mundane money was still a rarity, and I had lots of connections in Faerie.

"Plus," Grace added, "this is a pretty specific animal handling spell. I think we can trace it to the school of magic at least. That will narrow things down."

"Good," Patsy said. "Any chance I will get my money back?"

"Not likely," I said, "but I may be able to suggest a fitting punishment. Would you like them turned to frogs?"

"Vern!" Grace scolded. "That's not only cruel, it's not even possible."

"Maybe they should just kiss some frogs, then?" I suggested, and Patsy laughed.

"Toads, the warty kind, and you have a deal. Well, shoot. I really wanted this to be true—for Freidrich's sake as well as mine."

"Sorry we couldn't help more," Grace said and gave me a significant look.

I sighed. "Yeah. Sorry." I pushed the money across the desk.

But Patsy waved her hand dismissively. "Keep it. I didn't get the answer I wanted, but I did get the truth. Shoot. What do I do now? I monetized Prince Freidrich's social media. Got a line of merchandise, too. But now that he's a frog, I don't know. I'm going to have to give back the money I got on PleasFundMe that was for setting up Freidrich's kingdom. Anyway, I appreciate your time and honesty. And what you did, banishing that monster? That was badass. Kind of sorry I missed it."

"No, you're not," we both said hurriedly.

I rose, and we escorted her out of my office to the foyer. I was hearing shufflings on the other side of the double doors. On top of everything else, I'd have to go on a rat hunt before I could let Grace in the back area. The evening was just getting better and better.

"Can I ask one last thing, before I go?"

Without waiting for an answer, she pulled out her cell phone and a selfie stick, stuck Friedrich in the pouch between her breasts, checked her hair, and hit record.

"Hi, Freidlings! Freid and I are here in the office of DragonEye, PI, a real live dragon and his mage partner. These guys fought off an actual monster, so I figured, how much of a challenge can turning a frog back into a prince be after something like that, right? Unfortunately, Freid and I got the shock of our lives... It turns out – uh, what is that?"

She was staring at something in her selfie cam, but I'd heard the creek of the double doors. I turned around – and saw tentacles!

"Run!" I told Patsy and threw myself against the door. How in the world did Squidthulu get into my lair?

Unfortunately, I had weight but not enough bulk. The door hinges gave way on one side and the tentacled beast sipped through.

Patsy screamed and dropped her phone. Then instead of running like a sensible human, she did the Mundane thing. She bent over to retrieve it. The frog slipped out of her blouse.

"Freid!"

Grace opened her mouth to sing and got slapped in the throat by a whipcord of a tentacle. She fell back against the kitchen door and doubled over, clutching her neck. Ugly rasping escaped her throat.

Then it was chaos: tentacles flying, me snapping and ripping at any I could reach while I tried to force it back. Fried leaped and smacked at any that came Patsy's way, while she kept trying to catch him and was yelling at me.

"Careful! Don't step on Freid! Freid! Come here! Come to your princess!"

A tentacle reached for Patsy's outstretched hands. I smacked it with my tail. It swung in an arc and swept up her phone, somehow managing to knock it into my busted window, where it lodged in a corner.

"Now you're just showing off," I yelled at my wriggly opponent. It responded by grabbing my legs and snapping its bill at my abdomen. "Grace! I could use a little help here!"

Grace tried to talk and it came out as a squawk. She coughed and spat up blood. She looked from her hand to me with horror. Then, she grabbed the little table Bernadette insisted we needed at the front door and swung it with all her might against Squidinator's back.

It impacted with a wet *thwap!*, but the attack surprised it enough to let go of me and turn its attention to her. She dashed into the kitchen. Freid, meanwhile, chose that moment to start leaping from tentacle to tentacle like this was some obstacle course for its amusement. That confused it enough to hesitate, which gave me my chance.

I opened my mouth wide and bit down as hard as I could.

Patsy's shriek was almost as loud as the creatures. Still, it didn't stop, but reached back with two of its tentacles, grabbed me by the shoulders, and flung me toward the kitchen in a move that would have made a kung fu master proud. I was ready for it, however, and had my feet out to bounce off the door.

Unfortunately, my kitchen door wasn't up to my stunt. I crashed through. Squid Ninja still had a hold on me, and my fall pulled it, knocking the monster off its...whatever it was it was balancing on. At any rate, I heard the fwap and oof more than saw its fall.

"Freid!" Patsy screeched.

Freid? What about me? Figures. I spat out the chunk of calarevil I'd taken with me, then chomped hard on one of the tentacles still holding me. I struck with my claws at the other while my tail searched the counter for a butcher knife. Apparently 16 claws and 128 teeth were not enough for the job.

A horrid smell caught my attention and I noticed Grace in the corner pouring something into her mouth. The healing potion. It was brown and gloppy. Immediately, she dropped the vial and clamped both hands over her mouth, forcing herself to swallow. She looked green and woozy, but when a wiggly appendage came her way, she managed to duck. She grabbed a saucepan lid and held it like a shield. Her cheeks were puffed and her chest spasmed. I wondered if it would help to throw up on our attacker.

Back in the foyer, I was hearing grunts and more wet thumps. Sounded like Patsy had decided to take up the table. If she wasn't going to run, at least she was being useful.

Maybe too useful. Squidthulu suddenly released me. I heard a crash and a scream. I dashed into the room, Grace on my heels and trying to make any kind of clear sound. Patsy was crowded into the corner, holding the table like in those old lion-tamer cartoons, occasionally shoving it at the beak that snapped at her.

It grabbed the table and flung it away. I ducked.

Patsy screamed as the thing's mouth opened toward her.

That's when Fried jumped straight into it, his froggy legs splayed wide.

"Freid! No!" Patsy cried.

The creature jerked back. It started to twist and sway wildly, moving not unlike Sister Grace had just a few minutes ago. Whaddya know? It had a frog in its throat.

"Grace, get to the door!"

When it stopped and wrapped all its tentacles around itself in a squidish variation of the Heimlich, I dashed past to put myself between it and Patsy. Eyes on the creature, I started herding her toward the exit. I heard breathy notes coming from Grace. I was going to give her until it unwrapped itself before blasting it with fire. It'd probably take my house down. With my luck, Santry would consider it arson rather than self-defense.

The monster gave a great heave and popped Freid out of its throat. I caught it in mine. Patsy screamed, but before she could stop, I'd spun my head and spat it toward her chest. Freidrich apparently had had enough; he snuggled between her bosom.

I whipped back around, ready to let loose with fire, when Grace's voice returned. But rather than as something powerful and beautiful, what came out was powerfully loud.

The creature started to vibrate.

And then it exploded.

"Ew! Ew!" Patsy shrieked as we were covered in squid parts. "Oh, I'm going to be sick!"

"Me, too," Grace said weakly. She fell back against the nearest wall and slid to the floor. "I'm so out of practice with potions."

I looked around at what had been my newly cleaned lair. Blood and guts splattered the walls and ceiling and dripped off the door that hung ajar. The kitchen door was totaled along with the threshold. There were dents in the walls. Bernadette's decorative table now resembled some kind of modern art sculpture. In the window, a red blinking light said the camera was still filming.

While Grace groaned and Patsy cried, I walked over to the Corpsathulu and shoved it with my paw. Once I was sure it was dead, I sat back, bemused.

Looked like I was getting calamari after all.

Chapter Twenty-One: Nun of My Business

Princess Patsy
@Pasty&Fredirich

···

#Attackedbymonster - for realz! Freidrich saved my life.
He even jumped down its throat to choke it from within!
#notjustafrog http://dimtube.com/watch987rgal :o

♡   ⟲   ♡   ⟰

We stayed up until past midnight cleaning and packing minced monster in the snow to keep it cool. Grace managed not to vomit from the work or the potion she'd imbibed, but she was woozy. Our living quarters beyond the doors were clean (except the bathroom where we'd let Patsy shower) so once the worst was done, I sent her to her room.

The next morning, half-asleep, we picked our way into the kitchen for coffee and prayed the last day of the novena together. I wasn't sure if she was expecting an answer, but one had come to me, and I'd spent the rest of the night wrestling with it. The eleven weeks since meeting Grace had been eventful, and not just because I'd tangled with a dangerous foe and saved the world. That was becoming all-too regular for me. No, other forces were at play here, and I felt that the novena had brought guidance to me as well as Sister Grace.

Dragons, by nature, don't like being guided. In the past, we didn't need to be; instinct led us to do what was right. But that changed when my eldestkin succumbed to the sin of pride and dragged all our kind down with him. Now, instinct was clouded by selfishness, but eight centuries under the Faerie Church had taught me the importance of being obedient to the nudging of God. Yet was what I was considering really a nudge or just another selfish desire?

"You're awfully pensive," Grace observed.

"Last day of the novena," I observed in return. "Any thoughts?"

She leaned her head back against the chair, thinking, or maybe looking for strength from Above. She answered, hesitantly at first, but then with growing confidence. "Vern, I... I don't think you fully understand what the past couple of months have done for me. What you've done for me. I came here looking for someone to reassure me I wasn't crazy. Instead you, you brought me back to myself. Because of you, I'm reunited with my magic. With my voice. I haven't felt this whole since before I was captured. I never thought I would be this complete again—not in this life, anyway."

I shrugged, unsure what to say. I had thought she was crazy, more than once. Half the things I'd done were only because she was a client and later, because I was the only other person who believed her story.

It was more than that, said my own personal version of the Eye of the Resurrection. You went to her when you didn't need to. You defended her. You found a way to bring the lost lamb home.

I realized Grace was still looking up and not at me. "So, now that you are complete again, what do you want to do?" I asked.

"I'm not sure." She rubbed her cross like a worry stone. "Despite everything, I don't think

I'm ready to leave the Mundane." Her eyes drifted to the cupboard where her medications rested, reminders that her struggle toward healing was not yet complete. "I've no desire to return to the school, even if they would take me back. I'm fond of children—but only with small amounts of exposure."

I snorted. "I completely agree."

"So, what's a magic-wielding nun on the wrong side of the Interdimensional Gap to do with her talents?"

That was an opening if I'd ever heard one. "I have an idea."

I paused, suddenly shy. Did I really want to do this? Despite the advantages I could see for me, it had been a long time since I'd joined forces with a human. They were such frail, mortal things, and Grace was the frailest of all. Yet I also sensed the strength in her, just starting to come back to the fore. Even more, I felt we understood each other in a way others never did—not Brother Garken, not Joan of Arc, not even St. George.

As if to prove it, Grace didn't pressure me, didn't stare at me with expectant eyes. Instead, she rose and poured us each more coffee, giving me space.

I was able to fill that space with words. "We make a pretty good team. You handled yourself very well, not just with the monster but with the Patsy—"

"Vern," Grace scolded, but there was a hint of longsuffering humor in her voice. She understood the pun.

That decided me. "With Patsy and her froggy friend. Plus, you saved my skin against Squidthulu at the concert. We make a good team."

She shook her head. "I should have jumped in sooner, and I don't know how it got in through the repulsion spell."

"You got there in the end, and we saved the whole town. As for yesterday, I'm wondering if it didn't follow me home and take up residence before you came and set up the shield."

"Hiding, then, and absorbing magic? Aye, I suppose that rather than banishing it, I'd only knocked it down a size. I should have been more careful."

"Cut yourself some slack. It wasn't exactly my finest moment, either. We got there in the end."

"I suppose we did." She opened the refrigerator, pulled out a tentacle and set it in a pot of water to boil with a packet of Old Bay Spice that was in the drawer from before Señor Costa had died.

"Most of my cases involve magic. Why else would someone think of a dragon? It's not like I have natural brilliance and deductive skills or anything." I paused to roll my eyes. "At any rate, a mage would come in handy. Plus, having a human partner would open doors previously closed to me."

"You want me... to partner with you? As a detective?" She set my coffee on the table but forgot to retrieve her own cup before she sat down.

"It's not too different from the Inquisition. Somewhat more searching for missing pets, but I've had to save the universe a time or two."

"You get Save the Universes Cases?" she asked, and I could hear the capitalizations.

"Yeah, I get STUC that way," I quipped. Overtop her giggles, I added. "You have to know, the work isn't always steady, and the pay is not good."

"Perfect for a vow of poverty."

"So I'm reminded," I muttered. It was sore spot with me. What self-respecting dragon wanted to be impoverished?

"Could I remain in the loft?"

"Is that what we're calling that shanty of an office? Yeah, sure. I don't need it."

"How about some space in the warehouse to set up a proper workshop? I need to study. Obviously, my potion making needs work, and I'm sure there are other things I can create that will help in our line of business."

Our? "So... You're in? You want to do this?"

"Mm-hm." She smiled, excited and nervous. "I was actually up last night thinking about it. But there is one more thing. I need Tuesday nights off. I ran into the choir director at Adoration yesterday, and I asked to join."

"Advent!" Maria called out in a voice that could be heard across the pews. "A D B eN T."

Chuckles rippled across the church. Rita, both proud and embarrassed, shushed her toddler. "Pray now. Spell later."

"Later," she repeated. I reached over and tickled her with my tail before she could start spelling and incur the wrath of Mom. I was still on probation as trusted friend and caretaker of the Costa Cletch, so I was going to do anything I could to score points with Rita.

It was a relief to be back in the good graces of the Costa family and sitting at the end of the pew where eyes were as drawn to the size of their family as to the dragon that was bookending their menagerie. We'd rebonded over the past couple of weeks, with the whole family coming to my lair, armed with tools, lumber, and cleaning supplies to repair the front area and truly make Grace's new quarters somewhat loftier than they had been.

Bert and Natura chipped in. Bert brought some new screen to fix my door. Natura rolled her eyes at me, saying she was going to bring a beaded curtain that would do a better job, then Bert rolled his eyes at her. Natura did bring Grace some ridiculously colorful curtains she was changing out from the restaurant, as well as some cookware so we could make more than tea and microwave meals. Plus, they'd invited us to their Thanksgiving feast; we still had leftovers in the refrigerator. In the meantime, Ms. Patsy and

Freidrich's posts brought in several new clients. Apparently, she was not the only person to fall victim to Faerie scams based on Mundane fairy tales.

After Mass, there was the promise of coffee and donuts, then to the Costa's for Rita's famous chili. But what I was most looking forward to was coming after the First Reading.

We expressed our thanks to God, and the reader stepped down from the podium. Sister Grace rose from the choir and took her place. Her face was radiant with anticipation, and I felt my own heart soar. Everything that had happened this fall—that stupid song, Addison's lies, even getting my ribs broken by an oversized appetizer—it was all worth it for bringing Grace to this moment.

The piano played the introduction. Then Sister Grace of God, with joy, peace, and just a touch of siren magic, sang, transporting us all to a place of praise.

Siren Spell

I first wrote this story back in—wow—2012. It was my first attempt to explore Grace's past. There are times when a character wants to narrate, not like Vern, but with straight-out storytelling. This was one of those times. I really enjoyed letting Sister Grace tell me the story as if I were her grand-niece. Surprisingly little changed in the story between then and now. I was so glad to explore the deeper and somewhat darker ramifications of her past in this novel.

All right, child, stop levitating the crab and come to me. Yes, lev-i-ta-tion. That's the spell you're doing. But God didn't mean for crabs to fly, so let the poor thing back onto the sand.

Did God make you to swim? Well, that's the question your mother has asked me to find out. Sit down and pray with me, and then the Holy Spirit can guide me in this. Be good, and perhaps you'll be swimming with your sisters soon. I have a story to tell you—but first, stay still.

No, this spell won't make you swim. What? No, it won't make you a nun like me. Where did you get that idea? Well, Gells doesn't know everything, even if he is a griffin. God has a purpose for you, and you'll learn it in time. But for now, hush.

There, was that so hard? Now I'll tell you a story from long ago.

Paddy McCarthy was a sailor, a strapping lad, the pride of Aerie, with eyes the color of clover and a temper to match his flaming hair. They say, in his youth, he broke as many hearts as he did jaws. The sea took his hearing, but it could not take his spirit. Even stone deaf, he was signed aboard the Bonnie Brigit, and he made his living with hands on the ropes and his feet on the deck.

They were making a run of spices and dyes from Constantinople when the storm blew the

Brigit off course. They could see an island, tall and rocky in the distance, but the captain became fearful and screamed at the men, and they fought the direction of the wind until a fierce gust ripped the sail clean off the boom.

The crew struggled to free those trapped under it when suddenly, they simply stopped—and to a man, turned and ran to the prow. Paddy tried to stop them, tried to get one to face him and explain so that he could read their lips. But they wouldn't turn, and all he could see was, "the singing!"

They were heading to the rocks, and there was no one to stop them. As he tied himself to the mainsail, he watched in horror as men joyfully leaped overboard to their deaths. He didn't think even God could hear him in the storm, yet he prayed with all he had.

Aye, his prayers were answered, for he awoke on the beach. What's more, he was untied, and his head lay in the lap of a beautiful woman. Her hair was silver as the moon on the waves and her eyes were the color of the Medsea on a clear afternoon.

Gave him a start, she did! He was sure he'd died and gone to heaven. Ah, but then the sea he'd swallowed came back up his throat and the sand fleas made themselves noticed, and he knew he was alive and washed ashore on the island they'd seen. Only then, did he remember the old stories and knew where he was.

The Island of the Sirens.

Well, he was such a curiosity that the sirens let him live. They tried to sing to him; ah, but he couldn't hear a sound of it, and of course, she who found him protected him. Soon, he was accepted. Perhaps it was only natural that the two should fall in love. It does seem to the way of things.

The island was lovely, and he was well treated. For a time, he was content.

Then there came another storm—not as bad, but the siren gathered to sing. He could not hear them, yet the scene chilled him, and he ran to the shore and tried to pull them away from the beach, from their mission of calling ships to their doom. They turned on him, and only she whom he loved was able to keep them from rending him to pieces.

He was no longer welcome, nor would he stay if he were. The next day, he started to build a boat while the one he loved watched and mourned from a distance. Already deaf to her cries, he turned blind eyes to her tears until finally, she left him alone. Oh, sure, his heart was breaking, too, but he couldn'a stand to watch these people he'd come to think of as friends turn into the monsters their natures called them to be.

Still, he could not bear to leave the one he loved without a final goodbye. He searched the island high and low, finally ending up on the beach where he'd first awakened to her beautiful face; and there he found her, half-dead and feverish, her throat torn open. Through gestures and drawings, she made him understand that she had sacrificed her voice for the chance to be with him.

What did he do? He nursed her to health, of course! Then, they set sail toward the setting sun, then north. She swam beside him for most of the day, and lay beside him in the cool of night, gazing upon the stars.

They went to Rome, where they found a mage of the Church, who was able to return a portion of her voice, though it would never have its otherworldly effect. He bound her to land and the human form. 'Twas a painful process and her eyes paled to the blue of the sun-burdened sky. Yet she could not be lovelier to her dear Paddy. She was baptized into the Church, and the priest gave her a name: Cecilia, for the patron saint of music.

She agreed to raise their children as human and Catholics, and so they were married in a little chiesa by the sea. Before they embarked on a passenger ship to Dublin, the priest cautioned them: Though her form be human, her blood be siren, and that blood would pass to their children and their children's children. If they would keep them human, they must keep them from the sea until after they had received the Body of Christ.

So they returned to the land of his birth. His adventures had dulled his taste for the sea, so Paddy took over his family's farm far from the sea.

Cecilia was welcomed, though no one in the family or village understood her strange ways, nor why she looked toward the sea or the rising sun with such longing. But she came to love her new people and their ways, and when she sang at Mass, people would swear the angels had come to sing with her.

They had a boy, Mick, with his father's hair and his mother's eyes. They celebrated his First Communion by the sea, where they finally explained his unusual lineage.

Mick grew into a fine, strong man and took a trade as a smithy, traveling about the countryside making fences and railings. He found himself a wife, a sweet girl from a neighboring town. Brenna was but a serving wench, paying off her family's debt and not hoping for much more in life than to marry a poor farmer; Mick was sun and moon to her. Cecilia agreed to give her blessing on one condition: that their children never touch the sea until they received the Body of Christ.

"That is my requirement and the only dowry I demand," she said.

Brenna's family was too poor for a dowry, anyway, and she did love her Mick, so she gladly agreed to the strange request. When she was heavy with child, they explained the secret of Cecilia's past.

They had two children, Ian and Brigit, and lost three afterwards. Brenna turned to lacework as a way to cope with her grief, and soon was creating pieces of incredible complexity and beauty. She began, too, to suggest designs to Mick. Soon their works were the talk of three counties.

Finally, many years later, they had a daughter: a bonnie lass with silvery-red hair and eyes like the Medsea on a clear afternoon. She was the delight of her grandmother, who cared for her while Brenna worked, taking her to church and teaching her to sing. When she was but three years old, she sang "Ave Maria," Just those two words, over and over, and the priest wept for the beauty of her clear voice.

While their work was well-known, the village was too far from trade routes to bring in much money, especially for such fine artisanship as theirs, and Mick began to talk of moving to a port city, where they would find a better market for their wares.

Cecelia spat at her son and accused him of placing greed over the welfare of his children. In shame, he laid aside his plans.

Then a traveling mage visited the town, seeking a gift to please his bride-to-be. The children ran into the store while he was looking at Brenna's intricate gowns, and immediately his head snapped up like a hound catching a scent. He turned to the toddler peeking from behind her older sister's skirts.

"That one has power," he said. "Great power that must be trained, and soon." He told Brenna the schools in Dublin would have the best people to train their exceptional child.

That decided it. They would move—and soon.

"Who will care for my granddaughter? Who will protect her from the sea?" Cecilia cried, and such were her entreaties that they nearly relented; but in the end, Mick, stubborn as his father, stood firm. The older two had made their First Communion; they would find a house deep in the city; with the child busy with lessons and their home away from the shore, she did not need to know of the ocean for a few years.

Cecilia made them promise again and again never, never to let the child near the sea. They even took the more arduous overland route rather than sail along the coast.

But times change and people forget. Ian and Brigit were sent to fine schools, and the youngest had morning lessons with a tutor from the Magical Academy of Dublin. She also took singing lessons and her instructors were fair impressed with the quality of her voice and the way magic seemed to respond to it.

City life proved expensive, however, and Mick and Brenna had to work long hours. With the older children in school and Brenna in the shop, afternoon care of the child was given to a nanny who immediately questioned the unusual restriction against the beach.

Brenna would never hurt her husband or their family by revealing what she through of as their tainted lineage, so she merely protested that it was the will of the Church and had to do with a "condition" in the family. The nanny, however, scoffed at a priestly mandate given two generations ago.

"The sea air is healthy. It will help the child grow," she insisted to the mother. Month by month, Brenna's protests grew weaker and weaker, until the nanny felt safe in disregarding this silly rule.

And so, when Mick had gone to fetch his parents for a visit, and Brenna was busy in the shop, she took the four-year-old to the port. She had a new suitor, a fishmonger with a gentle heart and a booming laugh who loved children, and she wanted to impress him with her ward.

The sea called to the child. The lapping of the waves sang to her blood, so as her nanny and her beau laughed and spoke of things she did not understand, the child worked her hand free and followed the siren's call of the waves.

By the time her nanny noticed, the child had removed her clothing and was well away from the shore, instinctively seeking the currents that would take her south. The fishmonger swam after her, but even his strength could not make up for her speed; he finally turned back and nearly drowned, such was his exhaustion. They were sure the child was gone.

In fact, the child had seen a pretty boat and made her way toward it, swimming with unnatural ease. Equally unnatural were the sounds that flowed from her throat. Yet a child, she coaxed no man to leap to his demise, but all were drawn to the inhuman beauty of her song.

Then, Splash! There was another by her, familiar and strong. Her Da!

Rather than embrace her with joy, as she'd expected, he pulled her under the water. She struggled, but fighting to keep his own breath, he held her down with his legs and an arm across her mouth as he fished in his pocket. A rosary was wrapped around her neck and suddenly she felt confused, scared and heavy!

He pulled her sputtering to the surface.

"My child!" he yelled. "That thing tried to take my child."

They were pulled aboard, and under the instructions of her Gran, buckets of clean water were poured over her until she was shivering but no longer wet with the briny water. It didn't remove the longing, however. She had to return to the sea! She cried and struggled. It took three people to keep her from flinging herself overboard. When fighting them did not work, she sang, sang to make them give her what she wanted.

'Twas a riot she started on the deck of that boat. A riot, started only with a mere song; and the fighting did not stop until her own grandmother knocked her unconscious. Only by the grace of God was no one killed.

The child's magic and heritage proved too powerful a mix for the secular mages; only God could help her—and protect those she loved.

Sleeping draughts kept her controlled until they could take her to the motherhouse of Our Lady of Miracles, a convent high in the hills. When she awoke, she found she could not sing, and could only speak in a rasping whisper. A powerful spell had taken her voice.

Everything else was taken from her as well—her toys, her fine clothes, her family—until she had naught but the sisters. For a long time, all she felt was anger and confusion. She did not remember what had happened. Nothing the sisters said made her understand why her family had left her in these walls of stone. The sound of the wind in the trees made her yearn for the ocean. The sisters were patient, bearing her anger, then holding her when anger turned to tears. When at last she accepted her place, the work began.

They taught her the Catechism, endless drilling until she knew it perfectly and understood it as one older than her six years. On the day of her First Communion, she was allowed to see her family again, but already she was learning that this was only temporary. Over time, she began to understand that she had changed. The sea had awakened something in her. Unlike her siblings, she was not safe.

She begged to be allowed to sing and was told the Holy Spirit would return her voice when she was ready.

She was given a new name, Grace, for communion brought her grace—grace to be patient, grace to learn, grace to focus her increasingly growing powers. For many years, the sisters taught her only control and Catechism. When she mastered these, they moved on to holy magic. She received her Confirmation at ten, yet her voice remained trapped, and that night, she wept.

She continued her studies and grew in her love of the sisters and the order. When she turned fourteen, her family again made the trip to the isolated convent—this time to see her take her novice vows.

Her one relief from work was the letters she exchanged with her family. Encouraged by her mother and the sisters, her siblings wrote to her regularly; first short, awkward letters, then as they grew to be better friends, long missives full of their adventures, thoughts and dreams. Her brother Ian had followed in his granddad's foot-steps—wild and independent, he had chosen the life of the sea, signing aboard the Emerald Dawn which followed the Oriental routes. His letters were filled with descriptions of exotic lands and drawings of bizarre animals and birds. He claimed to have seen a dragon, flying high above their ship, indifferent to the awe-struck gaze of the mere mortals below.

Her sister Brigit took after her mother and joined the family business. When Brigit fell in love, she begged for her little sister to attend the wedding. With two of the order, who traveled as guards as much as company, Grace returned home for the first time in ten years.

Amid the bustle of the preparations came even greater news—her brother would return home for the ceremony! Anxiously, they counted the days till his ship docked and speculated on what presents he would bring.

The day of his expected arrival, the clouds brooded, but the breeze blew gentle and warm. By the afternoon, however, clouds turned the day into night and the wind screamed as it whipped through the trees. Her mother leaned against her father, and he kept whispering, "I'm sure they found port elsewhere."

No one believed it; the storm had come too quickly.

The family gathered to pray, but Gran asked Grace to help her retire to her room. Alone in the quiet, she looked the young nun in the eyes. She knew how they called to her: the storm, the sea. Her brother.

"You know what you must do," Cecilia told her.

Grace snuck out the window.

Standing alone on the pier, the wind tearing at her habit, she strained for some sign of his ship.

She saw it—a flash of tattered sail illuminated by lightning, at the wrong angle to be heading to the safety of the bay. She watched, heart in her throat, as they moved farther off. She prayed as the sail blinked smaller.

She sang.

Hesitant and scratchy, then clearer and stronger. Words she didn't know, words wrapped in magic and yearning. Words that threatened to take her over. She flung herself into the direction of the wind and let the rain slap her with the force of a beam. She shuddered, fought for control, and tried again.

Come to me. Come to safe harbor. The handmaiden of God calls to you. God is with you. The light of the world. The light of my song. Follow the song and find safety.

Wind buffeted her, rain blinded her, but it didn't matter. Time lost meaning. All that mattered was the song.

Then the Emerald Dawn crashed into the pier, and she went sprawling. A fierce draft of wind caught her and flung her onto the hard, rainsoaked sand. She saw lightning, then stars, then nothing.

She awoke the next day, her sisters—those of her blood and of her order—sitting worriedly beside her bed. When she opened her eyes and asked for her brother, she found herself smothered by arms and cries of joy and chidings and blessings until they all dissolved into laughter. Then her brother burst into the room and the entire scene was repeated.

Ah, but it was a beautiful wedding, with the bride as radiant as could be. They moved inland and had six fat, happy babies. Grace became a full sister, and a High Mage in the Church. But her siren blood, brought to life in her childhood encounter with the sea, ran full in her veins. While her siblings, then her nieces and nephews, all grew old or died, leaving their children behind, she aged far more slowly, time etching its lines upon her face with the patient persistence of water upon stone.

She never again used her voice in the way she had when saving her brother, but the call of her lineage remains a specter, a dangerous temptation she continuously fights to control. However, as long as she stays faithful to God and the rules of her order, she can use her magic and her siren's voice to do good for the world.

Aren't you the perceptive one? Yes, I am the child of the story, Grace, daughter of Mick and Brenna, granddaughter of Paddy and Cecilia, who communed with the sea before her Communion with God. Now don't cry. 'Tis a happy story, for I love my life and my Calling, and I've had more adventures than my brother ever did. No, I've never seen a dragon. Perhaps one day.

And there's a happy ending for you, too, great-great-granddaughter of Paddy and Cecilia. You see, Paddy and Cecilia never thought to ask the priest if he meant that Grandmother's heritage would no longer be a threat after three generations. And now the spell has shown me that the siren blood has been thinned by the human. Oh, you'll still have a lovely voice, but you'll never be siren.

Now off with ye. Go enjoy the water but stay close to your mother! The sea has other dangers, you know.

Ready for more Vern Fun?

Join Vern and Sister Grace on their first Christmas together in Christmas Spirits.

Acknowledgements

I had a short story, "Mishmash," which I had written for the anthology *Book of Tentacles*, which formed the basis for this book. I love anthologies because they give me great ideas!

As usual, my crit group, the CWG SFF authors were with me every step of the novel. They helped with some of the details (like Officer Tracy being there when Indira wanted to commit Grace). They were instrumental in helping me with Operation Trapison. It would have gone a very different way otherwise. (We've not seen the last of Addison, if I can write fast enough.)

My Beta readers again provided excellent suggestions enthusiastic support. Vern commends their great taste: Deborah Cullins Smith, K. Ann Seton, and Paul McDermott, who demanded "work as an unpaid proofreader" did an awesome job of catching my homonym mistakes (rein/reign, etc.) I used to be so good at them, but now, I write fast and read faster, and I get them confused. Can I blame it on punning? Re-gardless, he was a huge help.

Finally, Corinna Turner (who writes awesome dinosaur stories) noted that the "falling action" was awfully long. That's the part after the concert where everything is getting resolved. She (like me) is a self-professed impatient reader and thought there should be more action. So the Re-turn of Squidthulu is thanks to her. Vern thanks her, too. He got calamari, after all.

About the Author

Karina Fabian has been writing science fiction and fantasy since the early 1990s, when she left the Air Force after the birth of her first child. Since then, she's published over 20 books, been in numerous anthologies, and helped found an international writing organization, The Catholic Writers' Guild.

In 2020, when the rest of the world decided to stay home, eat too much, and practice social distancing, Karina – who already stayed home, ate too much, and was an old hand at social distancing – decided to start self-publishing so she could get all her stories out of her head and in the world. After clearing out her manuscripts, she's managed to publish two or three novels a year and hopes to keep up the pace until the characters cry "uncle!" To support this habit she writes product reviews for Fit Small Business.

Karina is married to Rob Fabian, the Chief Operations Officer for Vaya Space, a genuine rocket company. They live on the Space Coast where they can watch rockets launch from their front yard. They have four adult children, two dogs, and a multitude of migrating birds that feast in their yard.

Keep in Touch

If you want to learn about future books, please
- Sign up for my newsletter for exclusive Vern short stories, Space Traipse fun, updates and a free book! https://fabianspace.substack.com/subscribe
- Visit my website (https://karinafabian.com)
- Follow me on Facebook: https://www.facebook.com/Karina-Fabian-Speculative-Fiction-with-a-Grin-2233839790277963
- Follow *Vern* on Facebook: https://www.facebook.com/DragonEyePI

There's More Fun in FabianSpace!

Thank you for buying this book. If you enjoyed it, click to see the others in this series or discover one of the other worlds of FabianSpace.

Science Fiction

Space Traipse: Hold My Beer: Redneck ingenuity and common sense in a Star Trek-ish universe. Enjoy the adventures of the *HMB Impulsive*.

The Rescue Sisters: Intrepid women doing dangerous missions in space for the love of God and humankind.

The Old Man and the Void: Dex is a relic hunter on the edge of the black hole, desperate for the catch of a lifetime.

Jovian Heat: As the next Great Storm of Jupiter rises, Cass must find the father of a baby in peril—but the father died before the child was conceived.

Fantasy

DragonEye Story: Vern's a snarky dragon on the wrong side of the Interdimensional Gap, solving crimes, battling evil, and saving the universes on an all-too-regular basis.

Madness of Kanaan: Deryl isn't crazy; he's psychic, and aliens of two worlds thinks he can save them. Maybe he can—but can he regain his sanity in the process?

Horror

Neeta Lyffe, Zombie Exterminator: Neeta's an average exterminator, taking out bugs, rodents, and the undead. Can she keep her friends alive, pay her bills, and find romance?

Frightliner and Other Tales of the Supernatural (with Colleen Drippé): Truck-driving vampires terrorizing the road, Southern women doing what needs doing, a zombie wedding—a great story collection for horror lovers.

Twenty Words

Twenty words
That's all it takes
To leave a review
What a difference it makes!

Twenty words
What did you like?
What made you laugh?
What made you cry?

60,000 words
A year's work and plenty
Went into this book
Can you give back 20?

Please leave a review. It makes Vern happy, and it keeps the books on Amazon's radar, which makes me happy.